Leila's Truth

Deanna Reneé

PublishAmerica
Baltimore

First printing

ISBN: 1-60610-106-4
PUBLISHED BY PUBLISHAMERICA, LLLP
www.publishamerica.com
Baltimore

Printed in the United States of America

For Jade and Trista, my precious girls.
Thank you for making me smile every day.

-1-

The water rushed down over the windshield in one sheet. There was no way of distinguishing one drop from the next. All that was visible in front of me was the faint red blur of taillights. They seemed so far away. They were my only guide, and then, they were gone. I felt as if I was searching for a piñata, my arms outstretched, my eyes blindfolded, and feeling for something, anything. Tiny white lights rushed past my left, blowing their horns as they came closer. With my eyes squinted, I tried to see a bit more of the road, but realized that I could barely see in the night as it was. What little there was to be seen was blurred out by the downpour. I wanted to pull over and hope for the rain to slow, but I was so unsure of where the edge of the road sat. I may have already been in the gravel. I slowed my car to a mere eight miles an hour. At that point, I was shaking and sweating profusely. I was unsure whether my clothing was drenched in sweat or soaked from getting to the car. I gripped the wheel so hard that my fingers stuck to it. I looked straight ahead into the blackness. For as long as I could remember, I had been terrified of the dark. I reached for the door locks. I could not hear the clicking of the locks over the sound of the rain. It sounded like static from a television, but louder than any that I had ever heard.

I continued to drive until I had no choice but to stop. There were no longer any white lights. I hadn't seen any for quite some time. I knew that something was definitely wrong. I took that road only once before and I didn't recall having to make any turns off of it to get home, but yet, it seemed too empty, even with the heavy rains. Had I gotten lost? I decided that the only thing I could do was to sit and wait out the rain. As much as I hated the idea of sitting in a dark car, alone in an unfamiliar place, I knew I could not drive any further safely. It was a miracle that I had gone as far as I did without smashing into another vehicle or guardrail.

I pulled my Le Baron slowly to the right, hoping that I was on the shoulder. There was no way that I could be sure. I reached for the radio knob. I knew I couldn't allow myself to sit there left to my own devices or I would make myself even more terrified. I was like a child when it came to being in the dark. I got very nervous and paranoid, as if something were watching me from the shadows. I had to have a distraction. I closed my eyes and sank back into my seat, trying to make myself unknown to a possible onlooker. If anyone was out there, I wanted to make myself disappear.

"Hungry Eyes" played on the radio. I felt somewhat comforted as I visualized Baby and Johnnie dancing together as they did in the movie. I grabbed a hair clip from the glove compartment and pulled back my wet hair. I tried to take a deep breath. The air was so heavy that I could barely breathe. I cracked the window ever so slightly and put my lips up to the tiny rush of fresh air. It felt so cold in my throat, but refreshing. As I breathed in, I smelled something unfamiliar. It was an unusual scent that I could not seem to associate with anything. No one else probably would have noticed it, but my sense of smell had always been exceptionally keen. When I was young, my father used to refer to me as his little bloodhound.

On one occasion, he brought flowers home for my mother and she placed them in their bedroom. When I came in from playing down the street, I asked my mother "Did Daddy get you daisies today?" Although it was nice at times, the ability was not always enjoyable. The foulest of odors were almost impossible to overcome.

The odor that caught my attention as I sat in my car was very faint. After a few moments of thinking, I decided that it might have been a type of cologne. I wasn't altogether sure. It was a bit inviting, and I found myself reaching for the car door, ready to open the lock and get out. As my fingers rested on the handle, I peered out the window in both directions. On either side was darkness. Nothing moved, as far as I could tell. Of course, if something had been creeping around out in that rain, the probability of me seeing it through the downpour was slim. My body was tense as I sat with my nose to the window. The urge to go into the rain grew stronger. I imagined myself getting out of the car calmly as the rain began to ease. At that moment, the radio station cut out and I heard nothing. I snapped out of the brief trance that I had fallen into, and let go of the handle immediately. I twisted the knob on the radio back and forth a few times and pressed all the preset buttons. When I was unsuccessful at finding any further music, I gave up, and leaned back in my seat.

"Don't be ridiculous, Kate," I told myself. "You can't get out here. Who knows what could happen to you." I rolled up my window, closing off the small bit of ventilation that I had, and closed my eyes again. The static was easing up now. I could make out the sound of individual drops hitting the roof. Soon I would be able to return home, to the warm confines of my apartment, and bury myself between my three down pillows and plaid comforter.

As I turned the key in the ignition, I reached for the headlight knob and turned. The beams were brighter than ever. The rain had washed away the mud that once covered them. I looked straight ahead; ready to pull forward, when something caught my eye. There was a quick flash, like a piece of metal caught in the light of the beams. I stared into the weeds for a few moments, hoping to see it again, and then another flash occurred. Whatever it was, it was moving. I again felt compelled to get out. I imagined what would happen if I was to get out of the car, only to see that it was a wild animal. The scenario that played out in my mind was frightening, yet did not discourage me. Scared or not, my unfounded interest in the shine was enough to make me rationalize getting out of the car. If I was quick enough, I could jump out, see what it was, and get back into the car without catching too much more of the rain. It had eased up considerably at that point, but was it worth it? Why did I want so badly to get out of the vehicle when I was still so afraid? I was debating what I should do until, once again, I saw another quick flash.

"That's it. If I just look really quickly, I can be done with it all and head on home," I said aloud to myself. "It's probably nothing anyway, and I'm getting myself all worked up over something stupid."

After approximately five minutes or so, I was finally ready to get out of the car and look. I surprised myself with my unwarranted courage, as I was normally the type of person who would turn around and run in the opposite direction. Never before would I investigate the unknown, but I felt as if I had no choice but to look. I cautiously opened the door, mere inches at a time. I peered out through the open space, and then continued opening it another few inches, until the door was wide open. My feet touched the soggy ground and I stood. The mud oozed all around my shoes and even reached the bottom of my jeans. After pausing for a moment, I began to walk in the direction of the headlights. My heart pounded as if it was going to burst right through my chest. Even in the cool rain, I was burning. The sweat seeped from my palms and ran from my forehead. I could taste the saltiness as it streaked past my lips. I came upon the area where I had seen the shine and I swallowed hard. My teeth clenched and I felt a knot forming in the pit of my stomach. I regretted leaving the safety of the Le Baron, but it was too late at that point. I slowly lowered myself down to the ground before parting the tall grass with my hands. I gasped for air and dropped to my knees as I looked into the weeds. Before me were two water-filled eyes staring straight into mine. A small girl sat in a once pink dress, then saturated with mud, with her arms wrapped around her knees. Adorning her neck was a charm on a chain. The tiny silver charm was a dog.

-2-

We arrived at the hospital at eleven twenty-six p.m. The staff whisked away the little girl for examination immediately and I gave the head nurse what little information I had. I was asked a multitude of questions, none of which I could answer very informatively. I told them everything I knew about the girl, which was not much. She looked to be about five years old. She had not spoken a word since I had found her, but a bracelet on her left wrist had an inscription -***for my Leila***-.

Detective Malone of the county police force was the first to question me. He seemed bothered by the fact that he had a new case to look into at such a late hour. His hair was receding and he had the scent of an old man who had been sitting on a bar stool for too long. It was not an alcoholic smell, but that of stale cigarette smoke and greasy food. He entered the lobby doors, took a glance in my direction as he spoke with the nurse, and then came toward me.

"Good evening, Miss. I am Detective Malone with the county sheriff's office. I understand you are the one who found the girl along the roadside. Is that correct?" he began.

"Yes sir. My name is Kate Beach. I was on my way home from dinner, uh, with my folks about an hour out of town, when the rain became so heavy that I had to pull to the side. I thought I was lost, somewhere off the main road, so I uh, I waited until the rain eased up before heading home." I had a hard time calming down and the words were hard to come by. "Just before I pulled onto the road, I saw something shining in front of the headlights so I got out and looked. That's when I saw her." I recalled the night's events to the detective. He looked at me with crooked eyebrows.

"You know it's not safe to be out along the road at night don't you?" He said it as if he was talking to a child. "What made you get out?" he questioned further.

"I was terrified to leave my car, but a strange feeling came over me, like I just had to look, you know? That probably sounds stupid but it's the truth. I never felt like that ever in my life." I pushed the hair back from my eyes. "Is she going to be okay? Are her parents coming to be with her?"

Malone answered me in a very tired voice, "Well, it's too early to tell much of anything. She's being checked out now and it will probably be a while until we know more so why don't you, uh, well, just go home. Head home, rest, and I'll be in touch with you tomorrow if I have any more questions for you, and I probably will." He said it as if a wave of despair had just washed over him, as if the whole thing was an inconvenience to his life. He asked for my phone number and jotted it down on his tablet as I told him. With that done, he turned and walked out the door without saying a word.

I turned around and looked for the nearest chair. My legs were so tired from being tense while in the car that they burned. My entire body was void of energy. I thought about how rude the officer was to me. Go home, I thought. How could I go home? There was no way I would even be able to think about anything else, despite how uncomfortable I was. I wondered how the detective could be so nonchalant about what had just happened. Maybe it was a usual occurrence to find small children along the roadside. Despite his advice, I decided that I would at least stick around until her parents arrived. That way, I could relieve some of my worries once she had family looking after her.

I must have sat there for at least three hours without hearing a word from anyone. I had not seen anybody enter the waiting area or heard anyone asking about the girl. The silence was disturbing as I sat alone, looking around me. I approached the nurse station, hoping to see someone around the corner that I assumed led to an office. Someone had to be there to give me some kind of information. Anything was better than sitting there knowing nothing.

"Excuse me, ma'am," I blurted out when I finally caught a glimpse of a woman walking down the hallway. She gave me an awkward look, and continued walking casually. I assumed that she didn't much care for the sudden outburst, but I needed to make sure that I had her attention. It might have been another hour before anyone else appeared. As she approached the desk, I noticed her badge. It read "Pamela Brandt."

"Can I help you?" she asked as she began to scribble on a chart she had carried with her.

"Is there any news on the little girl who came in a few hours ago? I'd really like to make sure she is alright."

"Let's see, let's see," she mumbled as she flipped through a few pages. "Okay, here she is. You want to know about the little girl who came in tonight, right?"

I wondered if she didn't care enough to listen to me when I asked, or if she was overly tired from working night shift. I decided to give her the benefit of the doubt and assume the latter. I simply nodded my head in accordance.

"Everything checked out ok from what I can see here, but we are going to keep her for a while. That's just standard procedure. It also seems that she is afraid to tell us anything so, well, to be honest, we can't even figure out what her last name is. That's going to make it pretty hard to figure out what happened to her tonight. If you would like to see her, I don't see any reason why not." She paused, and then leaned closer to me and whispered. "Please, though, do not push her to speak. Any severe trauma like this can cause a child to be catatonic for many years thereafter. Believe me. I have seen it happen more than once. If that happens, we may never know what went on tonight."

"Of course, I understand."

The nurse pointed me in the direction of room 628, where the little girl laid alone, waiting. It was the children's wing of the hospital, so the usual hospital smell was missing. Instead, the scent of carnations and sweet bubble gum filled the air. A hospital is a scary place for anyone, but for a child, so innocent and unaware, it can be completely terrifying. I walked past pictures taped to various doors. There were sketches drawn in magenta and green crayons, markers, and colored pencils. I came upon door number 628. A drawing of a tree house still clung to the door. The previous patient must have forgotten it. I slowly opened the door. I peeked inside, trying to remain quiet so as not to disturb her, but the door creaked with every inch it opened.

She sat up and stared into my eyes once again, only this time, those eyes were saying something else. I was not sure what, but they lacked the sadness that I had clearly seen in them earlier. She was calm, as if she had expected me to walk through the door all along. I made my way across the room and crouched down near her side. I wanted to ask her if she was all right, but I was so afraid. I had no idea what this little girl had been through during the night. The last thing that I wanted to do was to say the wrong thing and upset her.

She was only five years old, from my own estimate. Her perfect, straight blond hair came just to her shoulders and was clipped back on one side with a tiny flower shaped barrette. There was a tiny silver heart in each ear.

I looked at her and didn't know what to say. Then I remembered the bracelet.

"Is your name Leila?" I asked.

She continued to look at me but did not say a word.

I thought to myself, "This poor child, alone in the hospital and no family is here to be with her." I could not imagine what she must have been thinking. As I sat, hanging my head in disbelief of the entire night, I felt something soft on my hand. I looked up into her eyes. Those big blue eyes smiled at me as she took my hand and raised it to her face.

"Everything is going to be okay, Leila. I promise you," I told her.

She closed her eyes and rolled over onto her side.

I wasn't going to leave her until someone arrived for her, so I leaned back in a chair and tried to relax. I hoped that in a few hours I would have some answers to my many questions. Why would anyone have left a little girl alone along the roadside? How long had she been there? Most importantly, why had no one come to the hospital for her? Surely, there had to be a family member looking for her by then. So many thoughts crowded my head, but I eventually dozed off into a very light sleep. It was a time when all the sounds going on around you find a way into your dream. It was not very rejuvenating, but definitely better than no sleep at all.

I opened my eyes after what seemed to be only a few minutes. The room was complete darkness, except for the small bit of light that shone from under the door. The ticking of the clock was the only sound I could hear. I was very warm for some reason. The air in the room was extremely suffocating. I looked at Leila. She was still. It would benefit her greatly if she could get a sound sleep, especially after the night she had had. I was all the while becoming even hotter. I felt drops leave my forehead and reach my lap. My heart was pounding at an incredible rate, just as it had when I was driving in the rain earlier that night. I attempted to raise my hand to my forehead to wipe the sweat away, but could not. I looked down at my hands but found nothing. They felt restrained somehow. I frantically tried to move them but I was powerless. My arms were tingling as all the hairs stood straight up on end. A ghostly chill ran down my spine. I had no idea what was happening, and I was terrified. I opened my mouth to scream, but only let out a gasp of air. I was completely helpless!

"Excuse me, miss?" a soft voice spoke to me.

I opened my eyes to see a middle-aged woman smiling down at me. It was light in the room. I looked to my left. On the wall was an orange clock. It was seven forty in the morning.

"Oh, wow, I guess I fell asleep," I said as I rubbed my eyes. My mouth was so dry that the nurse could barely have heard me.

"Good morning, dear. I am the nurse on duty this morning. Are you family to this little girl?" she spoke.

I looked around the room. No one else had come. I was still the only one there besides the nurse.

"No, I'm not, although I wish I was. She doesn't seem to have anyone who cares to see if she is all right." I moved closer to the bedrail and touched her soft hair. "Never mind that though. She's alright, isn't she? Is she hurt at all?"

"She's just fine," the woman told me with a smile. "Nothing is broken or bruised, I am happy to say."

I lowered my voice before saying, "Do you know what is going to happen to her? I mean, if there is no one here for her, where will she go?" I asked.

"Well, that's not up to me to decide, but I assume that she will be put in some sort of group home until family can be located. We are only allowed to keep someone here as long as they are in need of our care. The poor dear, she must be so lonely and scared," she replied as she looked in Leila's direction. Then, she returned her attention to me in a cheerful tone. "If you'd like a cup of coffee or something, there are some vending machines down the hall to the left. If you would like something a bit more filling, you can take the elevator to the ground floor. There's a cafeteria down by the front entrance."

"Yeah, okay. Thank you."

"Poor, sweet child, so innocent," remarked the nurse before turning and leaving the room.

Leila still slept, so I decided to get myself a cup of coffee before she woke. I left the room and entered the hallway heading for the coffee machine. Just as I rounded the corner, I nearly walked right into Detective Malone. He looked as if he had just gotten himself up. A thin layer of fuzz covered his face. He obviously woke up in a hurry. It was either that, or he simply did not care much about his appearance as his hair was disheveled and his uniform wrinkled from head to toe.

"Well, I thought I would find you here. I tried reaching you at the number you had given me last night but I got no answer. You were here the entire night?" He looked into my bloodshot eyes, as if they didn't answer his question. I was so tired from my restless night.

"Yeah, I was here. Do you need me for something? I mean, I told you everything I know."

He scratched his head while scrunching his eyes. I think he forgot what he was going to say in the first place. I could hardly believe that guy was even a cop. I felt no reassurance that Leila's situation would be resolved, not with that man on the case. He didn't seem to have any concern about his responsibilities as an officer.

After a moment, his eyes widened, as if he suddenly remembered what it was that he wanted. "I checked out what little information I had on the girl, but I've got nothing. There are no missing children reports on file and no frantic parents calling the station. Parents and relatives have accounted for all the girls I could find in past hospital records, by her name. Were there any houses near the spot where you found her?"

"No, nothing at all. I didn't see anything for a few miles, at least," I told him. I thought of what the nurse had said to me just moments before. "Is she going to be put in a group home until you figure out this mess?" I asked, rather worried.

"Most likely, yeah," he said while yawning. That's our only option in a situation like this, unless we can find a foster home, and quick," Malone said as he flipped through his memo pad. "Usually though, what happens is this: the mother will show up after a day or so looking for her. She will give us some sort of story about how the kid walked away when she wasn't looking; when the truth is that the mother was too busy doing smack to watch her kid." He chuckled quietly to himself. He was obviously pleased with himself for knowing the usual routine. "Either that, or she was out turning tricks."

I thought to myself. The previous week I finished a photography shoot with people from a nature magazine. We went to a beautiful woodsy area just out of town where there was a towering waterfall and frogs croaking in the mist. I made enough money from that shoot to last me for a while. I could afford to take some time with this girl. I couldn't see any other alternative. She would be put somewhere with more unfamiliar people if I didn't take her home with me, and I felt that she had been through more than enough.

"What if I take her, just for now?" I asked the man. "She is more familiar with me than anyone else at this point."

"Oh, I can see the paperwork already." He paused. "You want to take her home? Do you realize what you're asking?" He looked at me with a strange smirk on his face, as if I were incompetent of something so outrageous. "Are you willing to put all that you've got going on in your life aside for this girl? You know, it may be some time before we have any answers and, who knows, she may be difficult for you," he responded.

Difficult, I thought. Had he even bothered to look at the girl that he was supposedly trying to help?

"I'm sure we'll be just fine," I told him. "Besides, I could use I little time away from my work right now."

"Well, I'll have to go to the station and file the appropriate paperwork with child services before anything is final. I'll get the necessary forms ready and if everything checks out, we can set her up to go home with you. I hope you realize what you are getting yourself into," he explained to me.

He must have thought I was too young to know much of anything. I was young, yes, but not a child, as he seemed to think. I was very capable of looking after a five-year-old girl.

"I'll be in touch." He left without even looking in on Leila.

That's just as well, I thought. She certainly didn't need him. I was there. I wasn't going to leave her. She needed to have someone who she could begin to trust, and clearly, no one else wanted anything to do with her, least of all, the person who left her alone in the middle of the night.

After peeking in her room, I found Leila still fast asleep. She was so exhausted. I turned back to the nurse station and spoke to the woman with whom I had talked earlier.

"You know what, I think I'm just going to head home to take a shower and get clean clothes. If the little girl in 628 wakes up, would you please tell her that I will be back in a few minutes?"

"Of course," she replied.

-3-

The day was foggy with a chilling wind. I glanced at the sky as I waited for the light to change. I only lived four miles from the hospital, so I could be home and back before Leila even woke. The light became green and I made a right turn onto Haggard Street. It was such a nice area of town, even on the bleakest of days. I had lived on that street for three years. I rented an apartment at the top of the hill and I absolutely loved it. There were giant maple trees along the entire front of my building and flower boxes full of marigolds on every window ledge. Lilac bushes across the street perfumed the air, and in the summertime, there were always kids riding up and down the street on their bicycles. In winter, kids and adults both would sled down the snow-covered hill because there was never much traffic on our street. Even though I only rented, I didn't ever want to leave.

I pulled my car into an empty spot in front of the building and stepped onto the sidewalk. There were very few kids that day. The air was cold, keeping most children inside for the morning.

I fumbled around in my pocket, searching for my keys. When I came up empty handed, I figured it must have fallen off somewhere. The lanyard attached to them had seen better days but I kept forgetting to replace it. I didn't see it as a problem, however. Everyone there knew me. An elderly woman on the third floor kept an extra key for me and, in exchange, I promised to take her some cookies every Christmas.

I got to the elevator and saw an "out of order" sign. That was strange, I thought. It was a newly built elevator, which they had just installed the previous spring.

As I made my way to the stairwell, I smelled mildew and rotting food. I guessed that the janitor must have been sick over the night and let things go. He rarely let a tree leaf remain on the lobby floor, let alone leave rotting garbage lingering somewhere.

Upon reaching the third floor, I knocked on the door of the elderly woman's apartment. There was no answer. I waited a minute and knocked again, this time louder. I heard footsteps, and then the door creaked open mere inches before the chain lock stopped it. Two eyes peeked out, saw me, and then slammed the door shut immediately.

I found it to be strange behavior from a friend, but the woman was in her seventies and sometimes got confused. She must have thought I was someone else. I knocked again.

"Mrs. Martin, it's me, Kate. I lost my key. I just want to get the key to my apartment," I called in to her. "Mrs. Martin? Are you okay?"

There was no answer and after a few minutes, I had no choice but to leave. I decided that I would just have to either go back later when she would recognize me, or find my lost key. I walked back down to the second floor and stood in front of my own door. I figured I might as well check it. Maybe I had left it unlocked. I turned the knob. No luck. It was locked.

I pulled my coat tightly around my waist and headed out to my car. I wasn't really sure of what I was going to do. The chances of finding my key seemed slim. I could have lost it anywhere during the night. As I thought about what I would do, I glanced up to the windows on the third floor. A woman's face was looking down at me through sheer curtains. When I saw her, she jerked away. I looked at my own windows. I knew I always kept them locked, so there was no way I would be able to climb up and get in that way.

I climbed back into my car and turned on the heat. It was getting much colder outside. The heater in my car was not the best. The whole car was old and needed so many things fixed, but I loved it. It had never let me down and was great on gas. It was also paid off, and I liked not having to pay a car payment each month. It freed up money for other things, like new lenses for my camera.

Without being able to get into my apartment, I headed back towards the hospital. I could only wait until later to get a change of clothes. I always kept a few things at my mother's house, but she lived about an hour outside of town. If I went that far, I would never have been back soon enough. A girlfriend of mine lived just two miles from where I lived, but she worked from eight o'clock in the morning until four o'clock in the afternoon all week long. The day was Monday, so that was not going to help me at all

Since I had only been gone a few minutes, I drove down to the police station on Bell Street to see if I could catch Detective Malone. The building I pulled up in front of was as worn and ragged looking as Malone himself had been that morning. There were three police cars parked in the lot next to the station and two officers smoking cigarettes on the front stairs. They were holding their hats to keep the wind from taking them right off of their heads. They nodded and smiled as I walked up the steps past them.

Upon entering the lobby, I saw a tiny woman sitting behind a very large marble desk. It seemed completely out of place in such a worn down building. There was a small corner table with pamphlets on it in the far right corner, and next to it, a water dispenser. Although I tried not to, my nose cringed at the smell of the woman's cheap perfume, blended together with the cigarette odor that wafted through the door every time someone entered.

Once in front of the desk, I asked, "Excuse me, ma'am. I am looking for Detective Malone. Is he here?"

"Yes, dear, I'll have him paged for you. Please, take a seat," she answered in a soft voice.

I sat on a folding chair beside the corner table. ***Criminal Justice: Serving our Society*** was the first pamphlet I saw. Apparently, I could learn how to be a cop while waiting for one. I assumed that this must have been how Detective Malone became a cop. He lacked any evidence that he had been trained otherwise. I picked up another piece of paper. That one was about rape. It claimed that seventy-two percent of rapes went unreported. I wondered how they came up with that number. After all, they hadn't been reported.

"I thought I told you that I would get in touch with you?" he questioned in a condescending tone.

I looked up into the detective's shaggy face and stood. I wasn't at all surprised at how rude he was.

"Yeah, but I was away from the hospital for a moment so I guess I just thought it would make things a little quicker to come on down here," I stated, ignoring his attitude.

"Well, come on back to my office. I just got here myself. I was just beginning to check your name in our database. Follow me," he huffed, and I followed.

We walked down a long corridor into a room filled with roughly twelve cubicles. Office, I thought. He wasn't even good enough for an office. I sat at yet another folding chair, watching Malone as he entered my name into the computer. I had expected that much, as I had nothing to hide.

"Child services have given the go-ahead for the girl to be sent with you as long as your record is clean. They frown upon us sending kids home with pedophiles these days," he said with a chuckle. He saw my blank face, and then continued. "Now, I am looking at your file here and," he paused, "oh here it is. It says that you reside at 1341 Bradley Lane in Raytown. Is that correct?"

"That is actually my mother's house but I am there an awful lot."

"Miss Beach, that is the address in our database as your primary place of residence. If you wish to change it, and I recommend that you don't, we will have to do further paperwork to verify your new address and, quite frankly, I don't want to do it. It will slow done this whole process and that girl may end up with someone else in the mean time," he complained to me. He really was the kind of guy who only did the bare minimum, just enough to get by.

"I guess I could stay with her for a few days," I said as I thought of my missing key.

"Who knows, you may find it beneficial to you with a child to look after," he implied toward my incompetence. "Everything else here looks good, so I guess you're in the clear. I'll just need you to fill out some forms here. The girls at child services will have some more paperwork for you as well, but we'll deal with these for now. I'll fax a report over to the hospital so they know you will be the one to pick up, uh, what's her name?"

Oh, how he disgusted me so. "Leila," I told him.

When I walked into the open air outside the station, I felt a sense of well being, as if everything looked so much clearer than it ever had in my life. I was excited about having Leila around. She was such a beautiful little girl and I wanted so badly to show her love and compassion, something I was sure had been missing from her life. I could hardly wait to go get her at the hospital.

I drove back, trying to keep myself within the speed limit. It was so hard to stay calm. I already felt so attached to her, even only knowing her for such a brief period.

As I approached the nurse station on the sixth floor, the same middle-aged woman from earlier saw me and came toward me.

"Detective Malone is faxing over papers allowing Leila to be released to me. Do have any idea when I'll be able to get her out of here?" I asked in anticipation.

"We just received that fax so whenever she's ready, you two can go ahead and leave."

"Oh, that was quick. Thank you so much. You've been a tremendous help." I smiled and headed to Leila's room.

As I pushed open the door, I nearly tripped over the little girl. She stood directly inside the door, dressed in a sweat suit given to her by the hospital, ready to leave. Her arm was outstretched, waiting for my hand. I put my hand in hers. I had never felt anything so soft. I was instantly in love with her and knew that I would do anything to keep her safe.

We turned and walked, hand in hand, out the door and down to my car. She didn't say a word, but she didn't need to. The look in her eyes told me everything I needed to know.

-4-

The day had begun to clear up as we drove out of town. The sun started to peek through the clouds and I could feel it on my face. Leila sat quietly in the seat next to me. She gazed out the window, watching the red and yellow trees rushing past her eyes.

The drive to my mother's house was roughly an hour long. I never minded the trip though because it was such a scenic one. The trees were gorgeous this time of the year. Once off the main road, there was no traffic. The road was only used by my parents. I would always go slowly down the dirt road so I could look at the trees and try to spot animals, unless of course, I was driving at night. Then I would hurry along to get out as quickly as possible. I had never known anything bad to happen in that area, but I still got scared.

As we approached the end of the dirt road, a small, light blue, two-story house came into view. It was my mother's. She kept three hanging plants on the porch in the summer, and now, they swung back and forth in the breeze with dead leaves hanging out of them. I always had to remind her to take them down. Beside the house was a small shed, the paint peeling off in different spots. Around back, there were piles of leaves that my father had raked up, with no intention of bagging them.

Despite my being grown up, there was still an old swing set next to an oak tree in the backyard. It was more rust than anything else, but still stood strong. I rather liked seeing it there, as it reminded me of my younger days.

We pulled to a stop and I got out of the car. I motioned to Leila with a wave and she emerged from the front seat. I took her hand and walked towards the front porch steps. She seemed relaxed and in no way anxious. I hoped she would be comfortable once she met my parents.

Mom was a typical mother. She had always stayed home with me while my father went off to work. She was fantastic in the kitchen. There was never a bad meal and everything was made from scratch. My favorite was her oatmeal raisin cake that warmed me up from head to toe, even on the coldest winter days. Mom also loved taking pictures, although she never did it professionally. I guess that's probably where I got my interest in it. We would lie on the living room floor and color when it rained, and when it was sunny, we would picnic on the grass for lunch. Once or twice a week, while I was away at school, she volunteered at the hospital. There she would follow the nurses around on their daily routines and watch them. She would help with minor things and clean up a little when they needed it. She enjoyed it because she learned from it, and Mom was always willing to learn new things.

Dad was a great father to me. He was always concerned about how I was getting along at school and whether or not things were bothering me. He never let me go to bed for the night without tucking me in and kissing my forehead. Dad was always up at five o'clock for his coffee and was ready to open his store at seven a.m. sharp. He never missed a day, not even when he was sick and weary. He never let it show when he was unhappy. He carried himself around as if things were always wonderful, even when they were not. His shop was a small hardware store in town where his father and grandfather had also worked. It had been passed down through the family, but since I had no brothers, my father was going to run it until he no longer could. Then I would step in and continue the business. Even though I loved photography, I couldn't bare the thought of the store being sold or run by anyone other than family.

I tapped on the front door before opening it and walked into the kitchen. I didn't like to startle Mom so I always remembered to knock first.

"Well, there you are! I was wondering when you were going to come back. Lunch is ready if you're hungry," she said as I came through the door. She looked at Leila and smiled. "Well, hello there."

"What are you talking about mom? I never said I was coming out today," I explained. She caught me off guard and I almost forgot that Leila was with me.

Mom looked at me with a raised brow. "Okay dear, whatever. Eat while the food is still warm."

She said nothing of Leila being there, and proceeded to put food onto plates for everyone. I pulled out a chair for Leila and sat down next to her.

"Mom, this is Leila. Leila, this is my mom and my dad." I watched Mom as she sat a plate in front of Leila and then sat down across from me at the table. "She is going to be staying with me for a while. In fact, we will both be staying here for the time being. I couldn't get into my apartment today so I'm going to have to see the manager about getting another key made. I lost it somewhere between last night and this morning. Only thing is, the manager is away in Phoenix for a week."

Mom put her hands to her head as if she was getting a headache, then looked up and smiled.

"Are you alright mom?" I asked.

"Fine dear, it's just been a busy morning for me." She looked at Leila and smiled. Leila seemed completely at ease with her and smiled back.

"Are you hungry?" I asked her. "Go ahead and eat. It's okay."

I had no intention of going into details with my family about how I came to be with Leila, not while she was in the room. I would wait until she had gone for a nap and then I could explain.

Mom seemed to be acting a little strange that day, unlike her usual self.

"Kate, where were you last night? I called your phone and got no answer. I was worried." she asked.

"I'll tell you about it later mom. Everything's fine, don't worry," I tried to comfort her mind. She was always worrying about me. I don't think she much liked me living on my own. Although I was grown, I was her only child, and she didn't like it when I wasn't there.

Mom just glanced at me, lowered her head down and sighed. It drove her crazy not knowing.

I looked at my father. Sometimes he liked to come home for lunch when Mom was cooking something special. Today she made ham potpie and a fresh loaf of bread.

"How are things going at the store today, Dad?" I questioned. "Selling a lot?"

Dad paused. He seemed distracted.

"Everything's going well. Mr. Thompson came in this morning and bought an armload of power tools. It seems his all went kaput on him at the same time. Bad for him, good for us, I guess." He glanced at my mom and then back at his food.

We ate the rest of the meal in complete silence. Everyone had acted so strangely. We usually laughed and chatted throughout the entire meal, but that day, it was as if I had to force them to talk. I decided not to ask, and they said nothing.

After eating, I took Leila into the living room. "Do you want to watch something on television for a little while?" I asked.

She looked at me, then at the TV. She still wouldn't talk to me, but I wasn't concerned. It would take a little while for her to warm up and feel comfortable talking to me. I turned on the television for her anyway and found a channel with cartoons on it. She stared into the bright colors and I returned to the kitchen.

Mom had already started on the dishes. I grabbed a dishtowel and began drying them. When I did, my hands began to ache severely. I had minor arthritis in them and since I hand gripped the wheel so firmly while in the car, it was acting up.

"Honey, have you spoken with Dr. Kensington today?" Mom asked me.

"Who? I don't know who you mean, mom. Don't you want to hear about Leila? It's quite a strange story, and sad nonetheless," I disregarded her comment about the doctor.

"Yes, Kate, but I'm really concerned about you at the moment." She gently put her hand on mine. "You need to get in touch with Mr. Kensington. He is a very good doctor and I know that he will be able to help you. Please, dear. I can see that you are in a lot of pain. Your father and I are both very concerned about you. Will you go tomorrow morning? I'll call him right now and see if he can squeeze you in first thing," she begged, desperation in her voice.

I had no idea what she was talking about. I thought for a moment and then realized that she must have been looking down at my hands. The pain in my hands and wrist sometimes could be quite strong. When I started drying dishes, she must have seen that it was bothering me. I had intended to make an appointment for the past month or so, but was too busy with work to get it done.

"Yeah, sure mom, I'll go," I replied, hoping to ease her mind.

She breathed a sigh of relief, smiled at me, and turned once again to her dishes. "Now what were you going to tell me about Leila, dear?"

I told her everything that had happened the night before. She didn't seem at all shocked. Perhaps she hadn't been listening completely. I mentioned that no parents had come to the hospital for her, and she seemed saddened.

"That's terrible, Kate," was all she could say. A solemn tear rolled down her cheek. She brushed it away with her sleeve and continued with the dishes. "Where is she now?" she asked.

"I turned the television on for her in the living room. She's watching cartoons," I told her.

Mom wrapped her arm around my waist and we walked into the living room where Leila sat. I loved the way she looked. She was absolutely breathtaking. Her hair was so silky and smooth, untouched by any of the things that so often ruin hair, such as dyes or blow-dryers. She was thin, but healthy. She definitely had the look of someone who was well taken care of, which made it even stranger that she had been left alone.

I sat down next to her and Mom on the sofa.

"Leila, dear, would you like to go out back and play on the swing set, as long as the wind isn't too chilly?" she asked.

Leila jumped to her feet in anticipation. That definitely sparked some interest in her.

We all got up and went to the rickety screen door on the side of the house. It led to a small stepping stone sidewalk that curved around the back of the house. Once outside, Leila played and ran as any kid would. She ran through the piles of leaves and climbed on the swing set as if she were a monkey. She was smiling, and that was what I wanted most. I wanted her to be happy. We sat out back for most of the afternoon until the sky began to grow dimmer and the wind became brisk.

"I think we ought to head in now. It's getting too chilly for her to be out here," said Mom as she stood.

"Leila, we have to go in now," I called.

She leapt off the swing and headed for the same side door that we had come out of earlier.

We entered the house and found that we had really lost track of time outside. It was nearly five o'clock and Dad would be home from the store any minute. Mom began to heat up leftovers from lunch to eat for dinner. I didn't mind the repeat meal. Mom made the best potpie I had ever tasted, and when she made a pot, I would always eat it meal after meal until it was gone. The scent of ham filled the air and I felt my stomach ache in anticipation.

Dad walked through the door and grinned larger than ever. He was obviously pleased with himself.

"Good evening, my dear," he said as he kissed my mother's cheek. "Girls, guess who's sales were over the top today? Anyone? Well, I'll tell you! It was me! It was incredible! Everyone in town needed one thing or another today," he announced.

"That's wonderful, dear!" replied my mother. "Maybe we can afford that new siding sooner than we thought."

Mom and Dad wanted to cover the worn paint on the house with siding, as they had for a long time. It was excessively hard for my father to repaint every few years. He was getting older and so were his joints. He was not comfortable getting up on a ladder anymore, nor did I like him doing it.

"Siding is just the beginning!" he exclaimed as he sat down to eat. It must have been quite an extraordinary day for him to be so excited. I rarely saw him this pleased, and I loved it.

We ate dinner and everything seemed to be back to normal, aside from having Leila there. Dad spoke more about his day and Mom told him about the squirrels she saw while out in the backyard. It was a lovely evening. I was glad that we could all come together for dinner and show Leila what a real family was like. From the smile on her face, I would have to say that she approved.

After dinner and a little bit of television, we all said goodnight and went our separate ways to get some sleep. I walked up the stairs with Leila to the room at the very end of the hallway. I pushed on the door ever so slightly and it swung open. Inside was my old room, from when I was a child. Nothing had changed. Mom has always joked about keeping it exactly the same as I had left it but I never believed her. My pink and purple comforter still covered the bed and the wall was covered with yellow daisies that my mom had painted so many years ago. The room had always been a comfort to me growing up. No matter what was going on in my life and no matter how mad Mom was with me, I felt safe and happy in that room. As we walked into it, I felt that same sense of well-being come over me again.

I pulled back the covers and Leila slid between the sheets. She grabbed a small blue stuffed dog that sat on the nightstand next to the bed and sank back into the pillow. The wind whistled past the windows and the branches could be heard scraping against the glass. I touched her silky hair and kissed her forehead before standing. When I reached the door, I turned and smiled at her.

"Goodnight, Leila. Get some rest and I'll see you in the morning," I told her as she rolled to the side and closed her eyes.

Upon returning to the living room, I tucked myself under a heavy afghan on the couch and shut my own eyes. I knew I would sleep soundly that night. After all, by no means could I call what I had gotten at the hospital, sleep. I laid my head on the pillow and was almost instantly asleep.

I heard the cuckoo clock go off at three a.m. It was too loud to ignore. I let out a yawn and pulled the covers over my head tightly, trying to get right back to my sleep. Then, there was a creak. It was enough to make me open my eyes under the afghan. I wondered if one of my parents had gotten up for a drink. I lied silently and listened to make out what the sound was. I heard it again and pulled the covers down from my face. I looked around the room, but only saw trees lit by the glow of the moon. My eyes opened wider and I sat straight up on the couch. The woods in front of me were dark. I could hear the bugs crawling and buzzing beneath the bushes. Behind me, I heard the faint sound of cars passing by on the road. I had no idea where I was, but it did not seem familiar. I stood and stepped closer to the brush and looked into the moonlit trees ahead of me. The air smelled of pine and an upcoming rain storm. It was quite a strong smell. I stood silently and listened again. A branch snapped somewhere out in the darkness ahead of me. There was someone out there.

I spun around like a top when I felt a hand press on my shoulder. My eyes were open so wide I could feel them hurting. There was no one behind me. My heart was throbbing and I was more scared than I could ever remember being.

Another branch snapped! Someone was moving in my direction, but why, I had no idea. I tried to move my legs to run but they felt so heavy. I couldn't move at all. I could feel the air rushing upon me as my assailant ran to me. I squeezed my eyes shut and turned my head. My whole body tensed as I waited for what I was sure was my final demise.

I heard nothing. I no longer felt the air moving over me. The bugs had ceased buzzing. I was too scared look, but I opened one eye ever so slightly and peered around me. I saw the cuckoo clock on the wall. It read four twelve. I was sweating. I peeled the afghan from me and sat on the edge of the couch. I felt as I if had just run a marathon. Sweat ran from all over my body and my heart was racing. This was the second disturbing dream I had had, for the second night in a row. I had no idea why they were happening so suddenly. They made absolutely no sense to me. I thought for another moment about what had just happened and then lied back down. I just wanted to get back to sleep. I stared into the darkness for a few moments until my body seemed to calm down, then shut my eyes once again.

-5-

A beam of bright orange light shone through the sheer mauve curtains and onto my eyelids. It was morning, and it seemed to come just as I had fallen back asleep. I forced my sleepy eyes open and stretched my arms over my head. I found it to be seven thirty as I looked again at the cuckoo clock. My dream during the night had robbed me any feeling of rejuvenation. I actually felt even more tired than I had when I had first gone to sleep.

Mom was already up and came cheerily into the living room carrying a cup of coffee.

"I hope that's for me," I wearily said as I took in the bold smell of the java. Even my worst mornings could be made to seem bearable as long as I had a pot of coffee to get my engine going.

"Of course, and it's just how you like it," answered Mom in her perky morning voice. She patted my leg and sat down beside me.

"You didn't sleep well?" she asked, already seeming to know.

"You could say that," I replied as I thought of the moonlit trees.

"Your appointment is first thing, at nine o'clock, so you better get ready after you've had your coffee," Mom went on. "I'll watch after Leila while you're gone."

I had nearly forgotten that I had told her I would go. I didn't think she would make an appointment so soon. I did not see the urgency in it that I should have had to go so soon.

"Mom, that doctor you had mentioned yesterday, what kind of doctor is he?"

"A psychiatrist, dear, just someone to talk to," Mom said in such a calm, soothing voice.

I wondered why she thought I needed to see a shrink. Had she somehow known about the night I had just had? My nightmares had become even more frightening, and I was afraid they would become worse. I shrugged my shoulders and decided not to fight my mother on it. I would go to the psychiatrist and at least tell him about my nightmares, if nothing else.

"Well, I guess it wouldn't hurt to talk about some things, but how did you know? I mean, I've been dreaming…" I started to tell her.

"A mother knows, dear. I can tell when you've got things bumping around in there," she said while pointing to my head. "You've seemed a little bothered lately, and Dr. Kensington is very good at what he does, and quite handsome, I might add," she said while winking at me. "Talk to him about things in your life right now and see what happens. It couldn't hurt. "

"I guess," I quietly said as I sipped on my coffee.

I arrived at the doctor's office at eight forty-five. It was a good forty-five minute drive from the house. The lobby was in perfect order and it smelled of pine cleaner. A small stack of magazines and the day's newspaper sat atop a coffee table in the middle of the room. On the wall hung a framed picture of a chimpanzee holding his head in his hands.

I approached the window separating the secretary from the lobby and found a sign-in sheet. The secretary looked at me, then back at her keyboard. She looked to be in her late teens, although I'm sure she was probably some years older. I scribbled my name and time of arrival onto the sheet and found a chair to sit down.

I felt somewhat silly being there. I was not really in need of a psychiatrist. Sure, I had had some unusual dreams, but other than that, I thought I was a fairly normal person with typical problems. Even so, I hoped that he would tell me something meaningful about my dreams. If he couldn't, I really didn't know what else I was going to talk about to this doctor.

There was an elderly man sitting three seats to my left. He wore a pair of navy blue slacks with suspenders slung over his shoulders. His shirt was a red and black plaid with a small stain on the front pocket. On his head was a trucker-style cap that read "Sam's Fishing Supply". He must have been in his eighties, I thought. I wondered what could possibly bother a sweet looking man such as that. He hummed quietly as he waited.

On my right, four seats away, there sat a boy in his teens. I guessed probably fifteen years old. He wore mostly black, with the exception of his shoes, which were bright red boots that went quite a ways up his leg. His hair was completely unkempt. It was full of grease and stunk of cigarettes. I could tell by his outward appearance that he most likely was trouble; disobeying the law and his parents. He probably ran with a bad group of kids, and that is why his parents had made him go see a doctor. He rolled his eyes upon seeing me, and shifted in his chair so as to face the opposite direction.

As I flipped through the pages of Gardening your life, a magazine with tons of landscaping tips, I heard my name. I looked up to see a woman holding a clipboard, glancing around the room.

"Kate Beach," she called.

"That's me." I stood and walked in her direction.

"This way please," she said as we went through the door exiting the lobby. "You'll be in this room here," she pointed into the room marked 2A. "Dr. Kensington will be with you in a moment."

I sat down on a forest green lounge chair with cherry wood trim and tried to get comfortable. It was a little bit chilly in the room so I wrapped my sweater around me tightly. The walls matched the furniture quite nicely, as they were a lighter shade of green. There were numerous certificates hung all around the room. I assumed that they must have been degrees and awards the doctor had received. I hoped that that meant that he was an excellent doctor.

After five or six minutes, the door opened and in came a man wearing a maroon sweater vest and khaki pants. His hair was very thick and wavy, and his face sported a goatee. He obviously did well for himself, as he wore a Rolex watch and a golden chain around his neck. My mother had been right. He was, in fact, rather attractive. I glanced at his left hand as he approached me and saw no ring.

"Good morning Kate. I am Dr. Kensington, but you may call me Steven if you prefer. How are you doing this gorgeous day?" he asked right away.

"Well, I'm alright for the most part. My mother is the one who wanted me to come here today," I told him.

"Yes, I talked to her last evening. She told me about what happened to you the other night and said that you may need to talk about a few things. Would you like to get started?" he continued.

I nodded and lied back on the lounge. I felt as if I was in a movie. I had never been to a shrink before and it was just as I had expected. It looked just as it did on television, when the patient lies back while the doctor sits in a chair behind the lounge. He started asking me some basic questions.

"Would you please tell me your full name and your age first," he began.

"My name is Katherine Elizabeth Beach. I am twenty-four years old," I told him. I heard the scratching of his pencil on paper. I wondered what he could possibly be writing about that.

"What is today's date and day of the week, please," he went on.

"Today is Tuesday, October 21, year 2000. I really don't see how this is going to help me," I began to tell him.

"I just like to establish a few facts before I begin the sessions. Go ahead and tell me what it is you would like to start with today and we'll delve into it," said the doctor.

"Well, I guess I'd like to know about the dreams I've been having," I started. "I've only had two, but they were pretty frightening." I could hear the pencil scratching once again behind me.

"When did these nightmares begin?" he asked.

"Just two nights ago was the first one. It was when I was in the hospital with Leila. She is the little girl that I found out in the rain." I told him about the dream that occurred that night and about how I felt restrained. He continued to write as I talked about the second dream and explained it in vivid detail. A chill ran down my spine as I thought of being in the woods again. It was still so fresh in my mind and it still frightened me a little bit.

"Who do you feel was after you in this dream?" he questioned when I stopped speaking.

"I don't know, but there was definitely someone, I know it. It was the eeriest feeling."

Dr. Kensington continued, "You'd better tell me exactly what happened the night these dreams began. Your mother told me what she knew, but I need to hear it from you. Tell me how your night began and lead into the events surrounding Leila's discovery."

"I was leaving Mom and Dad's house. We had eaten a big dinner together and then I left around eight o'clock to head back to my house. It is an hour drive to get home from there. I drove into heavy rains and I had to slow down considerably. After a while, the rain got so bad that I had to pull over and wait until it slowed down enough to get back onto the road." I proceeded to tell Dr. Kensington about the night and about how I found Leila. He continued to write on his notepad and occasionally said "hmm." He seemed to hang on my every word.

"You say you left your parents' house around eight, correct?" he asked to confirm his writing.

"That's right," I answered.

"And when did you reach the hospital?"

"It was about eleven thirty," I said as I thought of being at the hospital.

"That must have been a terrible rain to slow you down that much. I do remember rain that night but I didn't go out into it at all," he said to me. "Perhaps something happened within that time frame that is causing you to have these nightmares. Did you see anyone else that night, maybe someone was along the road walking and caught your eye?"

"I don't remember anyone other than Leila," I said. "I could barely see the road, let alone someone walking along side of it."

He looked up from his writing and said, "Sometimes our dreams are our mind's way of reminding us of places we've been or people we've seen. The dream that took place in the hospital may be to get you to resurface something you felt once before. The one from last night may be trying to lead you to the woods for some reason. Did it seem familiar to you in any way?"

"No, not at all. I have no idea where I was, other than in the woods, and that could have been anywhere." I said.

"I think that the best way to understand our dreams is to make them as real as we possibly can. Sometimes, once we do, other important information becomes available to us. I recommend that you go out and try to find this place from your dream. It doesn't have to be the exact place if you don't know of it, but make your surroundings the same as they were in your dream."

I wondered what exactly it was that he wanted me to do. It sounded as if he wanted me to walk in the woods at night, but I could not believe he would recommend something so unsafe.

"Of course," he continued, "don't go out alone during the night, but try and find where your dream took place. I think you'll be quite surprised at how much it will help."

I continued to talk for quite some time, although it only seemed like a few minutes to me. Eventually, Dr. Kensington stated that our time was over and I would have to schedule another appointment. He wanted to review everything I had told him and see me again in a few days. I was almost disappointed that our time was done. I felt somewhat relieved as I sat and explained everything to a total stranger. I wasn't sure how much, if any, he had helped me, but it was nice being able to talk about everything. Therefore, I agreed to another session.

I thanked him for his time and shook his hand before I left.

"It was good to see you, Kate," he said as I left the room. As I reached the lobby, I thought about whether I should really come back or not. Mom had recommended him, but I didn't see how I would be helped by following his advice and going into the woods somewhere. I already knew that I wasn't going to find anything out that I did not already know. I was afraid of being in the dark, and dark woods were certainly no better. I let out a sigh, and, despite my reservations, turned towards the secretary's desk to make an appointment with the woman there. I knew that if I didn't reschedule, I would have to argue over it with my mother once I returned to the house. She was very persuasive when she wanted something done. I knew that I would end up having to call the doctor's office as soon as I reached her house, so instead, I scheduled another session. I was just about to leave when the secretary's soft voice caught my attention.

"Have a great day Kate. We'll see you again soon."

"Thanks Ann. You too," I said as I left.

-6-

The day was much brighter and warmer than the previous one had been. I looked forward to taking Leila out to the trendy clothing shops to pick out some clothes for her. She certainly could not wear a hospital sweat suit all of the time. I had always thought that it would be fun to shop for little girls' clothes because they were just so adorable. Things were more colorful and stylish than when I had been small.

I pulled up to the house and thought of my own place. I hoped that the building manager would not decide to extend her trip, as I would be without a key even longer. I debated going back to see Mrs. Martin about getting my key, but she had acted so strangely the day before. I was a little nervous about trying again. For the time being, I decided not to worry about it. I always enjoyed staying with mom for a few days, and I know that she absolutely loved having me there.

I walked into the kitchen to see Mom making what would later become meatballs. It was only ten-thirty in the morning, but everything she made took so much time that she had to start early if she wanted it to be just right. She turned as she saw me coming in the door.

"Hello, Kate. How was your talk with Dr. Kensington?" she asked eagerly.

"It was okay, I guess. I don't see how it is supposed to help, though," I replied.

"Why do you say that? Did you talk about the other night and what happened?" she asked further.

"I did, but I don't understand what any of that has to do with my nightmares. I made another appointment, but I don't know. Maybe I shouldn't go. Dr. Kensington seemed to think that I should try to make my dreams real, by going to the places I see in my dreams. The thing is, I don't know where I was in last night's dream. I know it was in the woods, but that's all," I told her. "What do you think?"

"I think you should listen to the good doctor. He went to school for a reason, so he knows what is right for you. You're having these nightmares for a reason, I know that much," she continued to mix the hamburger meat. "Since you don't know what's going on, you owe it to yourself to find some answers. You don't want to have nightmares forever, do you?" she asked me.

"Certainly not, but I'm not sure where to begin," I answered with discouragement.

Mom was right, as she so often was. If I made some sort of an effort to make the dreams more real, then maybe something would come to mind.

"Well, the whole thing seems kind of silly to me, Mom. Besides, maybe it was just something I ate that didn't agree with me." I laughed softly as I walked past her.

"Don't be ridiculous, Katie. Keep your appointment," she said as she gently smacked my leg.

I strolled past her and into the living room where Leila sat with the stuffed blue dog from last night. Her hair had already been combed and was pinned back with a pink clip. She wore blue jeans and a red t-shirt with a kitten on the front.

I looked at her strangely for a moment, and then returned to the kitchen before Leila had seen me. I didn't recognize them as any of my clothes from when I was young. On the other hand, perhaps Mom had gone out that morning, while I was gone, to buy some clothes. I really hoped that she hadn't gotten too many because I was so excited to shop with Leila.

"Mom," I said as I turned the kitchen corner, "where did Leila get those clothes? I was going to go with her to pick some out today."

"Those were yours, Kate. Don't you remember?" she said as she crinkled up her brows.

"I don't think those were mine, Mom. I don't remember having anything with a print on the front. As a matter of fact, you know I always wore dresses," I said very assuredly.

"What does it matter Kate?" she said becoming slightly defensive. "At least she has something to wear. Now are you going to stand there or help me with these meatballs?" she asked, seeming eager to change the subject.

"Uh, I'm sorry Mom. I'm going to take Leila out for a while. We'll be back in a little bit." It was so odd seeing Mom irritated, especially over something so insignificant. I figured that maybe she had an argument with Dad, or perhaps one of her friends. Even that didn't seem to make sense, though. She seemed fine just moments before when I had returned from the appointment. I brushed it off as nothing and assumed that once back from our shopping excursion, she would be her normal self.

I retrieved Leila from the living room and we got in the Le Baron. I still wanted to buy her new clothes so we headed down the dirt path to the main road. We passed a small pond on our way out where Dad and I used to fish when I was twelve. The water sparkled as the sun shone down on it. A few tiny pink flowers still clung to the water's edge, apparently not ready to call it quits for the season. A large blackbird swooped in and out of the trees, cawing each time it came lower to the ground. I looked at the road ahead of me and watched the road signs whiz past as we drove.

"Leila, we're going to go shopping for clothes for you. How does that sound to you?"

She said nothing, as usual. I was growing accustomed to her silence, yet was looking forward to hearing what her voice sounded like.

"It will be lots of fun. Every girl loves to shop and I bet you're no different. When I was your age, I loved dresses more than anything. Mom used to get patterns and sew dresses for me; everyday ones and fancy ones for playing dress-up. Of course, she bought me some too."

Leila tilted her head toward me and gazed into my eyes. They were dark, glazed, and fixed on mine. Her expression showed sadness, and she shook her head in disapproval.

"What's wrong? Don't you want to go shopping?" I asked, but she continued to shake her head at me. What could have happened so suddenly to make her sad, I thought. Just moments before, she was happily looking out the window, smiling.

I looked again through the windshield. There was a figure on the right hand side of the road, quite a ways up. I watched as we drove closer, and the object came into view. It was clearly a person; a woman around my own age. I slowed my car down, so as not to hit her, and drove closer yet. The woman walked very slowly, and I wondered if her car had broken down somewhere. She looked ragged, as if she had been walking for a long time. I reached across Leila's lap for the lever to roll down the window. Any decent person would offer her a ride, at the very least. I looked past Leila's disapproving face out the window and saw something that made my eyes burst open wider than ever. My silhouette was staring straight ahead. In the instant that I looked, everything was in slow motion. My own face turned to me with a grim expression. It was a dark face, with bags under the eyes and an overall look of despair. Tears ran down her dirt-covered cheeks and fell to the ground. She glared at me with blank, disapproving eyes, just as Leila had, and shook her head from side to side.

My body shook with tremors and my jaw dropped. My heart skipped a beat as I heard a whisper. I saw the face saying something through the glass, but I could not decipher it. I threw my arm across Leila's front and slammed on the brakes. I screamed so loud that I didn't hear the tires screeching as they slid over the pavement. I gripped the steering wheel so tightly that my nails dug into the vinyl. My chest was thrust against the wheel with a thud. My head cracked against the dashboard and everything went black.

When I came to, I sat for a moment, perfectly still. I wasn't sure if I was still alive, as it seemed nearly impossible to catch a breath of air. I slowly opened my eyes after a minute or two and allowed them to focus. I saw the windshield intact, but the dashboard covered in blood. I remembered hitting it with my head and knew I must have been bleeding. I turned immediately to Leila. She sat hunched forward, held in place by the seatbelt, but not moving. I reached for her and touched her shoulder. I shook her gently and waited. Nothing happened.

"Leila," I said, quietly at first, into her ear. "Leila, please talk to me! Just look at me! Anything, please!" I began to scream at her. "Please wake up!"

She remained completely still. Her hair fell forward over her shoulders. She sat there lifeless, her head hung downward. Only moments before, she had been sitting, looking out the window. She had an entire lifetime ahead of her. Anything could have happened.

I put my hands to my head as the tears poured from my eyes. I could not comprehend what had just happened. I didn't know what to do. I looked to the rear-view mirror to see if the woman was still visible behind me. She was not. I wondered if I had really seen my own face, or for that matter, anyone at all. It had all happened so quickly, and Leila's young life was gone in an instant. I wiped away tears with my then mascara-stained hands and sat with my eyes closed. I was terrified to open them again. I wanted it all to go away, but I knew that I had to get out and find some help, so I pulled back my hands. After a few minutes of coaxing myself to open my eyes and deal with the situation, I did. When they finally opened, there was a large oak tree to my far left, like the one beside Mom's porch.

"Sorry to keep you waiting, Hon. Just a tub of butter and some black olives please. That should do the trick."

I turned my head to see my mother casually walking down the porch steps to my car. She saw the horrified expression on my face and the streaks of black from my make-up.

"Oh, Kate, are you all right? Baby, what's wrong?" she asked frantically. She threw open the car door and scooped me into her arms, holding me tighter than ever.

I said nothing, as I was still trying to grasp what had just happened. It was so real. I felt sure that it was not a dream, even though, clearly, my mother stood right in front of me. I could feel her arms around me, yet I was still reluctant to believe it all.

-7-

Mom lifted my feet up onto the sofa and covered me with the afghan my grandma had made years ago. It was nowhere near being a square shape and had every color imaginable thrown together in no particular order. Mom sat at my feet, rubbing them lightly.

"I think you should rest a bit," she said in a soothing voice. "Leila is coloring out on the kitchen table and I'll be out there with her. You relax for a while."

"No, Mom. I want to be with Leila. I can't relax anyway. I want to spend time with her. That's why I wanted to be the one to watch after her," I said as I started to stand from the sofa.

"Just sit for half an hour, okay?" Mom pleaded as she gently tugged on my arm.

"I'm fine, Mom, really." She looked at me the way that she did when I got into trouble as a kid. "Well, okay," I agreed, "but just for a little while."

I sighed, and then leaned back into the cushion in defeat. I would sit for a while but then I was determined to spend time with Leila. As of that time, we had not done much together, and that's not how I wanted her to remember me when she left.

I closed my eyes and tried to relax while Mom went to the kitchen. The disturbed visage I had seen earlier remained fresh in my mind. I remembered the doctor's advice about my dreams and wondered what he would think if he knew about that one. Make it real, I thought to myself. That was the last thing I wanted to happen. I had never been as terrified as I was when I thought that I had ended a little girl's life. Moments later, as I sat in silence, the phone rang. Mom picked it up and I strained to hear. I normally didn't eavesdrop on her, but I so desperately wanted to get away from my own thoughts. Relaxation seemed impossible with everything that was on my mind. I heard her say, "Yes, she's here." I knew she must have been talking about either Leila, or me and if so, I wanted to know who was asking.

"She's busy at the moment. Can I take a message?" There was a pause. "Oh, hello Detective Malone… Yes, okay, of course… Well, I will let her know… Okay… What's that? Oh, yes, she is fine… All right then… Bye."

I had not even gotten warm yet under the afghan. I leapt from the couch and dashed to the kitchen, where Mom and Leila both sat at the table, coloring in books.

"What did Malone want? He doesn't know about what's going on with me, does he?" I asked frantically.

"No, Kate. How would he know?" answered Mom reassuringly.

"I don't know. I just don't want him to think that I am not fit to care for Leila," I said as I slumped onto a chair. "He might put her with someone else if he thinks I'm crazy."

"Don't worry, dear. There's no way that he could know anything. All he did was ask if you were here and if you were handling everything all right. I told him you were, and that I would let you know he called. That is all. I didn't even realize that that was the gentleman who allowed you to take Leila. Had I known, I would have spoken to him about her," she went on. "And you're not crazy."

"Spoken about what?" I asked.

"Just that we enjoy having her here and would like her to stay," said Mom. "I mean, if no one steps forward as family to her, she could stay with us, right?" she questioned me.

"I don't know how it all works, but I am sure it's not that simple. If she stays with me, we'll be back at my apartment soon, not here all the time. What I do know is that that may not happen, Mom. There are probably a lot of technicalities to go through before they would allow me to keep her permanently." I imagined having Leila with me all of the time. It would be a lot of fun to have someone around who enjoys dressing up and having tea parties. I always wanted a sister for that reason when I was a little girl. Unfortunately for me, I had been an only child. "Nevertheless, I'm sure someone will turn up sooner or later. She must have some family."

"Well, she belongs here with me. I really enjoy having her around." She put her arm around Leila and squeezed her gently.

I looked at Leila. She colored perfectly within the lines of her picture.

"I don't think we should be talking about this around her any more. We've said too much already," I said as I ran my fingers through my hair.

"You're absolutely right. She doesn't need to hear any more," mom concluded our conversation and resumed coloring with Leila. I picked up the carnation yellow crayon and began coloring with them.

Dad swung open the front door at twelve-thirty and sucked up as much air as his lungs could hold. He seemed quite pleased with the aroma of the simmering meatballs and sauce. After pouring a cup of coffee, he sat with us. He loved the fact that, since he worked for himself, he could always come home for lunch and be with his family.

"There are my beautiful girls," he said cheerfully. "How is everyone doing today?" he asked as he looked at Mom, and then me.

My gaze turned to my mother. I sighed, and then nodded. I knew she hated to keep anything from my father, so I didn't want to put her in that position.

"Leila, why don't you go and wash your hands before we eat. It will only be a few more minutes," Mom said to Leila. Leila put down her crayon and went toward the bathroom.

When she had gone, Mom began. "Carl, Kate has been having these nightmares since the incident with Leila the other night. Today she actually had one while she sat in the car for a moment. You should have seen her! It was terrifying! I have never seen her like that before," she told Dad. "She was sobbing hysterically."

"I'll be fine Dad. It's nothing to worry about," I told him. I wanted it to seem like less of an ordeal than it really was. There was no point in getting him worked up when he had to return to work.

"Nothing to worry about? How could you say that? Of course, I'm going to worry. You're my little girl." He sipped the steaming cup of coffee. "Your wellbeing is my primary concern. Now, I think you ought to make yourself an appointment with Dr. Kensington. He'll be able to help you." he asked.

"You already know about him?" I was a little surprised. "Mom was telling me about him last night."

"Well," he looked at Mom for a moment, "he has helped a lot of people that I know, and I have heard good things about him. People talk when they come into the store."

"She saw him today, just before the incident in the car. I think that she should continue to see him for a while, don't you Carl?" Mom asked.

"Don't worry Mom. After what happened today, I intend to see him again. I want to figure this out so I'll stop having these nightmares. Had I already been driving when it started today, I could very well have killed us both."

"Don't talk like that, Katie. Everyone's fine," Dad scolded me.

"But it's the truth, Dad. I am really getting scared. I don't want to hurt that beautiful little girl. She has so much that she hasn't experienced yet in life, and I could have ended it just that quick. It's a terrifying thought. I just hope there is no way that Detective Malone can find out about any of this."

"Who's Malone?"

"He's the cop who arranged for me to bring Leila here."

"Why would he need to know about your dreams? What business is it of his?" Dad was getting upset at that point.

"Dad, I'm just afraid that Leila will be put somewhere else if Malone thinks I'm not capable of caring for her," I told him.

"You're perfectly able to take care of a five year old girl, dreams or no dreams. Those people don't know anything. You never mind them," Dad stated, confident of my abilities.

Leila entered the kitchen wearing her usual smile. She came to my side and took my hand. Her hair smelled of bubble gum shampoo, which reminded me of how hungry I was.

"I hope it's time to eat because I sure am starving. How about you, cutie?" I asked her as I heard my own stomach growl.

-8-

The sun set very slowly, and the sky gradually got dimmer. The beautiful pinks and oranges were becoming less and less. I sat on the porch steps and watched the brown leaves blow across the grass. The wind whispered into my ears. It may have been trying to tell me where it was going, but I couldn't understand. I pulled the hood of my sweatshirt over my head and tugged at the strings. I thought about the day's events over again in my mind. I thought about Dr. Kensington and everything he had said. Then, just for a moment, I forgot about everything and only saw his gorgeous face. I chuckled to myself at my terrible timing for thinking about a getting a date, then returned to the problems at hand.

The woods ahead of me were not yet very dark, and so the thought of entering them had crossed my mind. I imagined myself in my dream from the night before and wondered. Maybe those trees that stood in front of me would provide some kind of answer, or maybe I would end up scaring myself further. I was already afraid, and things were getting progressively worse. I had nothing to lose.

I tied the lace on my sneaker and stood. I felt somewhat ridiculous thinking that a stroll in the woods was going to solve my problems, but my options were limited. As I neared the edge of the yard, the wind again whispered to me. This time it was more like a warning. I began taking small steps and heard the leaves crunch under my feet. As I walked, I became calmer. I realized that it wasn't as bad as I had thought it would be. There was still some sunlight showing into the trees and I could see most of what was around me. There were bushes to my right that still had a few dried up berries clinging to their stems. Mom liked to use those to make jelly. It was my favorite kind. Ferns met up my left side halfway, and ahead of me was a mix of evergreens and half-naked oak trees.

I was much more at ease than I had expected. I began to walk at a normal pace. I continued to observe everything around me. Nature was so beautiful. It was something I had always loved. My favorite photo shoots were those that took place outside. Brightly colored flowers and meadows begged to have their pictures taken, and I felt honored to be a witness to such beauty.

I bent down to pick up a small branch from the ground. As I walked, I poked at trees with it and swung it from side to side. I kept thinking that at any time, something was going to pop out at me from the bushes, but nothing did. I continued to walk until I realized that I must have gone quite a ways into the woods. I decided to turn around so I wouldn't be stuck out there when it did finally get dark. I turned back and saw only trees. I was so far from the house that I couldn't even see the outline of it through the trees. I picked up my pace, eager to get back inside where there were no surprises.

I came to the edge where the yard met the trees and felt a sense of relief surge my body. I had expected something awful to occur out there, and it had not. I was completely fine and had had no strange happenings. That doctor, what does he know, I thought. Nothing came of me being in the woods. I sighed and walked up the steps leading into the side door.

Although I was relieved, I had almost wished that something would have happened. Instead, I was no closer to an answer than I had been.

Warm air surrounded me as I went into the house. It felt so comforting to be once again in the delicious smelling aroma of my mother's house. I slipped the sweatshirt over my head and slung it over the back of a chair. I glanced around the room. It was where Mom and Dad kept a small desk with a typewriter on it. There was also an old recliner in the far corner that Dad absolutely loved. He refused to get rid of it. When I was a baby, it was the only chair in which he could rock me to sleep. On the back wall was a beautiful landscape photo. It was a picture of a meadow with mountains in the backdrop. It seemed familiar to me. I had given my parents plenty of my photos over the years, but there was something about that one. I walked closer to get a better look and saw what had made it stand out to me. Not only was it mine, it was my very first published photograph. I cherished it more that anything else that I owned. I could not believe that it was hanging on my parents' wall. I hung it at home over the fireplace mantle, and that is where it has always been. I had no idea how it came to be hung on their wall.

I immediately went to the kitchen to find my mother. She sat at the table with the day's newspaper in hand.

"Mom, I'm not trying to be mean, but why do you have my favorite photo hung in the back room? You know that one is my pride and joy! How could you just take it like that, without even saying anything to me?"

"Oh my, Kate, calm down," began Mom. "There's no need to get angry."

"Yes, there is a need! You know how much I love that piece! How did you get in the apartment to get it anyway?"

"Kate, sit down dear. I know you're upset but let me explain, please."

I sat down at the table, infuriated that she would take something without so much as a word about it to me.

"Now, I know you think you had it at home, but there are some things you don't know about. It has been here for a long time," she said to me, "and, well, you have been, too."

"What are you talking about? I remember seeing it at my house before I came here to eat the other night. I know it was there," I explained to her.

"The photo is here because you have been living here for quite a while. You brought your things here and you set a few things around the house, such as your photo."

"That's ridiculous, Mom. I know where I live, and it's not here, as much as you would like it to be."

"Do you know what you said to me the morning you came home with Leila?" she asked, looking deep into my eyes. I thought for a moment.

"You said you had lost your key to your apartment and that Mrs. Martin wouldn't let you in. Do you know why she wouldn't let you in?"

"Mom, she's old. Sometimes she gets confused. And the key isn't a big deal. I can get another one made," I tried to make her understand.

"Oh, my sweet girl, Mrs. Martin probably doesn't live there any more. That's why whoever came to the door didn't let you in. Did you see her face?"

I thought hard about the other day. I hadn't actually seen Mrs. Martin, but had assumed that it was her. Nonetheless, I didn't see how that had anything to do with what Mom had been saying. I couldn't figure out why she believed that I was living there. I had lived on my own for three years in that apartment.

Mom continued, "I know all of this makes no sense to you right now, but it will. You see, well, how can I put this?" she paused for a moment to think. "A while back, you were having some problems with things. I don't know if it was work that was causing you stress, or what it was exactly. Anyway, my point is that you were really stressed about something and it seemed to be the root of problems to follow. You began to have moments when you would forget things. You would wake up one morning and have totally forgotten about the two previous days."

"I don't understand. How could I have forgotten about something as huge as moving back in here? Just the other day, I was in my apartment."

"You only think it was the other day, sweetie. See, we thought all of this was taken care of until you came in the other day and mentioned your apartment."

"Wait, just wait a minute," I said as I covered my face with my hands. "Why would I have suddenly forgotten a chunk of my life? That doesn't make any sense."

"Things in life so rarely do, babe. The doctors had said there was a chemical imbalance in your brain that could easily be fixed with pills. It was just something that derived from the stress. You began taking medication, and I asked you to move back in here. I thought it would be easier for you to get things back to normal. You never objected to it."

I found it hard to believe that I would have so easily given up my own freedom for my mother's peace of mind. I absolutely loved my apartment in town. The whole story of hers seemed ludicrous. How would a person forget pieces of their life due to being overly stressed? It didn't seem feasible. On the other hand, even if there was a slight bit of truth in it, I wondered how much I had forgotten. The images of my apartment were so fresh in my mind, as if I had only been there a few days ago.

"I don't know how I can believe all of this. If this is really what's happening to me, why have you let me continue to think this way? You should have said something the moment you realized that I had forgotten again," I said.

"Oh, Kate, I wanted to, but I couldn't. I wasn't sure how to handle the situation, since the episodes had been gone for some time. That's the reason I called Dr. Kensington. I told him what had happened and he told me not to tell you until you started asking questions. He said that it would be best for your own sake to figure things out on your own. Then you came in and started asking about the photo and I didn't know how to explain it to you so you would understand. I didn't want to keep lying because you were so upset about your picture. That's when I decided to tell you. Oh, please don't be cross with me, Kate. I only did what I thought was best for you," Mom pleaded with me.

I was in complete shock. Never had I been told something so detrimental, at least not that I could remember. It did make the incident at the apartment building make a bit of sense, but not enough so to convince me. There were two many questions to be answered.

"If this happened before, then why aren't I taking any meds for it now?" I asked Mom.

"The pills could possibly have had adverse effects if used for too long, so when you appeared to be better after a length of time, you were taken off of them. It seemed like the right thing to do."

"How often was I forgetting?" No, more importantly, how long have I been here? What day is it?"

"It's the twenty-first of October," answered Mom.

"Well, see then. That's the day I already thought it was."

"It's not the same year, honey."

"Oh, come on, Mom! You want me to believe that it's a year later!" I looked at her blank expression. It did not alter. "Has an entire year passed?" I questioned her in a softer voice.

She lowered her head and rested it in her hands. I heard her let out a heavy sigh. "I wish I could say that it wasn't true, but I just can't."

"You're telling me that I missed an entire year? That's what you're saying? That's impossible! How could that much time pass and I have no recollection of it?" I ran my hands through my hair as I paced around the kitchen. "This is too much. I… I just… I'm so confused. I can't believe that you're telling me all this," I began to break down in tears.

"Kate, you need to calm down for me sweetheart. I know this is coming at you so fast, but there is no other way to break it to you. You have to know what's happening. The sooner you understand, the better off you will be, and the sooner things will make sense again."

"I just…I can't process all of this at once. It's just…it's too much right now! How did…I mean, I was just there and… I don't know." I rubbed my head with my hands. "I'm going to go lie down for a few minutes before I tuck Leila in for the night. This is so messed up." I wiped the tears on my shirt sleeve. "Can you just leave me alone for a little while?" I asked her, my face twisted with confusion. "I can't talk about this any more."

"Of course, dear." She remained at the table, her face saddened. "Kate," she said. "When you're ready, I'm here for you."

I nodded and left the room.

I could not understand what had happened. It seemed impossible that I could miss a whole year and not even realize it. I felt fine, other than the nightmares I had. I thought myself a completely rational person, and certainly did not feel like I was forgetting pieces of my life. The whole idea of it seemed unimaginable. Along with the feelings of bewilderment, I also felt foolish. Everyone around me had lied to my face, treating me as if I were crazy. I must have looked so stupid to everyone around me, I thought. Dr. Kensington was in on the lies too. A complete stranger, who knows nothing of me, talked to me knowing that I had no clue of what was going on around me. I didn't know which emotion felt worse at that point, the anger or the embarrassment, or possibly the empty feeling inside of me. I obviously was not the person who I thought I was.

I still wanted some type of proof, something to verify Mom's story. She said I had brought my things to the house, but they were not in plain view, if they were there. I thought about when I was a kid. Mom used to hide all of my Christmas presents in a trap door that opened into a small room beneath the laundry room.

I went to the back room and looked at the floor. A green rug spread over the hardwood, covering the majority of it. I knelt down and pushed it aside. The door underneath was not locked, as it always was when I was a kid. Mom had always been afraid that I would fall in and get trapped in there, so she kept it locked at all times. I lifted the door and peered inside. It was dark, but I knew where there was a bulb. I climbed down into the darkness until I felt my feet hit the soft ground.

The room was cool and smelled damp. It was not a finished basement, by any means, but it was suitable enough for storage. I reached for the hanging bulb and turned it on. As my eyes adjusted to the dim light, I looked at everything surrounding me. On one side were a stack of boxes and a whole collection of frames propped up against each other. I knelt down to look closer and found all of my favorite photos, framed as they had been in the apartment. To my left were boxes full of knick-knacks and kitchen utensils. On the right, a shelf sat loaded up with all of my books on photography that I had always kept beside my bed.

My heart ached and my eyes welled up as I realized that everything Mother had said was the truth. I closed my eyes and thought of my apartment. It wasn't just the lost apartment that bothered me. It was everything that it stood for. It was where my life had turned for the better. I had become a professional photographer while living there. It was my freedom and a piece of who I had become. So much inspiration came from what I would see on a day-to-day basis looking out my windows. Just that quickly, it was all gone, and I didn't have a clue that it had ever happened.

I sat on my knees on the dirt floor, feeling the cold of the ground through my thin pants. I did not want to return upstairs. I was ashamed of my lost life. Apparently, I had become someone else over time and I had no say in the matter. Maybe, I thought, I still took pictures. Mom had not told me that I no longer did, she just said that I had moved back home with them. There became a small spark of hope in my mind, until I saw something else. A leather strap dangled from another box on the ground. To my discontent, I reached into it and found my camera. It was dusty and worn, thrown to the side just like a Christmas tree after fulfilling its holiday duties.

I tried to hold back my emotion, but found it impossible. I was so proud of everything I had done with my life, and there it lied, packed up in boxes never to be seen again. Tears dripped and made a small bit of mud at my feet. I pulled myself up and turned back to the ladder. I had seen all I needed to.

I climbed back up into the laundry room and saw Leila sitting on the floor, apparently waiting for me. From the expression on her face, I could tell that she was worried. I quickly wiped my tears so as not to let her see me cry, knowing that she had already caught me. I picked her up and she surprised me with a great big hug. It was warm and comforting, so much that I felt a little relief. I set her down and we went in the living room and sat in the recliner together. I pulled an afghan over us and she snuggled up against me until she got comfortable. With all the chaos that I had just found out about, all I wanted to do was relax and go to sleep. Tomorrow was going to come and I would worry more when I woke. We gazed at the television for an hour or two. Leila went right to sleep, and when my mind quit racing, I followed after.

-9-

The scent of crisp bacon and scrambled eggs with cheddar diffused through the air. I poured a tall glass of orange juice for Leila and took a seat at the breakfast table. My dad had already left for work, so Leila, Mom, and I were all together for breakfast. I filled my mug to the brim with piping hot coffee, leaving just enough room for a packet of sweetener. I felt much better having had a good night's sleep. Leila and I had fallen asleep on the recliner and I never woke until morning. Nonetheless, the chair had been comfortable and I had no nightmares. I felt a little more at ease than I had the evening before, when my whole world was thrown through a loop. I didn't feel quite as helpless as I had. Perhaps because I felt like my normal self, regardless of what my "normal" actually was.

"How well did you girls sleep last night? I noticed you two asleep in the recliner. You didn't stay there all night, did you?" Mom asked as she took a sip of her juice.

"Yeah, we did, Mom. I never woke up during the night or else I would have taken Leila up to bed. She must have been tired too. When I woke up, she was laying just as she was when we went to sleep," I told her.

Leila seemed plenty rested as she was happily swaying back and forth in her chair as she ate her eggs. She still had not said anything, but was cheerful at least.

"I don't recall having any nightmares last night, Mom. I slept the whole night through. I know I really needed it, too. I feel refreshed this morning, in spite of everything you told me."

"That's wonderful, Kate. I am so glad that you are feeling better. Once everything settles in your mind a bit, you'll feel even more at ease. It will just take some getting used to." She scooped eggs from the pan and put some on both Leila's plate and mine.

"I would like to get the camera back out of the basement, though. I can't figure out why I would have boxed it up in storage anyway. I can still take pictures no matter where I live. Do you know why I chose to stop, Mom?"

"Maybe you just couldn't find as much time for it anymore. I'm not certain, dear. It was just something that gradually faded from your daily routine. Oh, don't forget, you should probably contact Dr. Kensington today so you can get back on that medication for a while."

"What's the point? I mean, it didn't cure me, so why should I get back on it?" I asked Mom.

"Because it helped, that's why. You didn't erase the problem, but you don't have any other options. You can't continue this way. What if you wake up tomorrow and forget everything? Then I'll have to tell you all over again and you'll be devastated once again. Medication is the only logical solution here, Kate. It worked before and I know it will work this time too."

"I don't know, Mom. There has to be a way to eliminate this all together. It doesn't seem right that I should just have to deal with the fact that I may forget my entire life at any given moment. If it was gone once before, maybe it could have been gone for good. Something may have triggered its return again. Perhaps if I talk to the doctor regularly, I can beat this," I attempted to convince my mother. "If I get to the root of the problem, maybe it will take care of it. Besides, didn't you say that it started because of stress?"

"Yes, I did, but I can't say for sure what is really making this happen. I have no medical license, Kate. I'm just calling it how I see it, and the way that I see it now is that you should see the doctor and do whatever he recommends. He has been following you through this entire ordeal and knows what works and what doesn't."

"I don't know, Mom. I think pills are just a cover-up for people's problems. I'd rather not be on meds for the rest of my life anyway."

I stood to retrieve more juice from the refrigerator when the phone rang. I answered.

"Hello, Kate speaking."

"Kate, this is Detective Malone. How are you this morning?"

"A tad early, don't you think Detective?" I asked a little surprised.

"I apologize, but this is the only time I'll have free to call you for the entire day. I'm swamped today. Anyway, I'm just calling to find out if everything is going all right. Does Leila seem to be content staying with you?"

"Yes, we're doing just fine. Leila is happy from the looks of it and my parents really enjoy having her here. It has been wonderful for me as well. I'll be sad when it comes time to send her home."

"Well, that's part of the reason I'm calling," he continued.

"Oh, really?"

Mom looked up at me. Her face showed her concern about the reality of sending the little girl away. I know she had gotten attached to her since she had arrived.

"I have been doing all I can to locate anyone related to her and I've come up with nothing, time and time again. I've checked out all birth records in the entire state for girls born between four and six years ago and I've found absolutely nothing. Now maybe she was born in another state, and if so we'll find out, but it may take some time. I've got a few other detectives helping me check records, but we can't check forty nine other states in a day."

"If you're wondering how long I am willing to keep her, you don't have to. She can stay as long as necessary," I assured him.

A wave of relief came over my mother's face.

"That's great. I thought you would say that. I'm going to have my secretary send you a few things that I forgot to have you sign along with some papers from child services. I'll check back with you again soon. Is that all right?"

"That's fine, Detective. I'll be here if you need to speak with me again."

"Thanks, and have a great day. Sorry about calling so early."

I hung up the phone and stood. My face must have given away something, as Mom stared with wondering eyes.

"What's wrong? Did he say something upsetting? What is it Kate?"

I was in shock over how polite he had been to me. He was a very different person than he had been the other day when we spoke at the station. Maybe he was having a bad day before.

"Everything is fine, Mom. It's just that he was actually nice to me on the phone and, well, I wasn't expecting it. He even asked about Leila. Quite frankly, I thought he couldn't care less. Anyway, she is staying for a while so don't worry about that," I said as I looked into her eyes, "and that's all that matters."

She flashed me a toothy smile and went right back to her breakfast. She didn't seem to be concerned about anything, just the way a child should be.

"Let's celebrate with some more juice," Mom said as she topped of everyone's glasses.

As I ate, I thought about the day's events. I still had yet to take Leila for some clothes, as I promised her the day before. If it wasn't too chilly, I also wanted to take her along the old paths that I used to walk. There were paths through the trees that led back to a creek in the woods. I had walked those beautiful trails many times. It was so relaxing to see nature at that time of the year, when the leaves were colored so wonderfully and bright. When thoughts weighed heavily on my mind, I would walk back to the creek and sit atop a large rock overlooking the water. I would toss pebbles into the stream and forget all of my troubles, if only for an hour.

We finished breakfast and Leila went to get dressed for the day. Mom had laid out some more of my old clothes for her on the bed upstairs. I followed up the steps behind her and headed for the hall closet. I kept a few of my own clothes there for times when I stayed overnight. I swung open the folding door and saw a wavering stack of clothing. I quickly rose up my arms to keep them from toppling down on me. I held the clothes in place with one hand and selected the day's attire with the other. I had not realized there were so many things at Mom's house, but soon after, I remembered that it was once again my house also. I sighed as I was reminded of my lost independence, and then closed the closet.

The hardwood floor was cold under my feet as I stepped down the hallway. The room where Leila was staying was at the far end. I peeked into the open door and saw her sitting on the edge of the bed, pulling up her socks.

"Well that was quick," I quietly said to her. "You go ahead downstairs if you're ready. I'm going to pull my hair back and change clothes, so I'll be down in a minute or two. Then I'll comb your hair for you and make it look nice. Okay?"

She smiled, brushed her hand against mine as she passed, and went down the stairs. Today, she wore a purple dress with a white sweater over the top and white leggings. It fit her perfectly and she seemed quite pleased with her appearance. That dress I had remembered well. It was my absolute favorite. I knew Mother would keep that one because it had meant so much to me. I wore it every chance I got, and sometimes fell asleep in it at the end of the day. Despite all the wear it received, it looked beautiful on Leila that day. I smiled as I saw her leave the room looking so happy. I loved that she was enjoying it just as I had.

I entered the green bathroom beside my old bedroom and began to clean myself up for the day. As I brushed my hair, I stared at the woman I saw in the mirror. She looked different to me that day. My eyes seemed tired and my face looked older than my twenty-four years. I kept brushing and realized that I was actually twenty-five, since I had missed an entire year. I was, in fact, quite awake that morning, but it was not apparent as I gazed into the mirror.

I finished up in the bathroom and returned to the kitchen where Leila and my mother sat. Mom was drinking coffee and Leila was having another glass of juice.

"We're going to go out today. Do you want to come along, Mom?" I asked.

"I've got so many things to do today, Kate. I promised Mrs. Flynn, the woman next door, that I would make her apple cobbler today. She loves it so much, but can't seem to get it to turn out right when she makes it. I also have to make a pie for the church banquet tomorrow night. That reminds me, are you two going to go with me?" Mom asked eagerly.

"Sure. I don't see why not, but do I know anyone who will be there? I mean, will I remember anyone?"

"Most of the folks I've known for years, so I'm sure you'll remember some from when you were little. Besides, I'm sure they would love to see Leila."

"How do they know about her?"

"Well, I spoke with Mrs. Flynn yesterday and I mentioned Leila, and Mrs. Flynn's mouth is hard to keep shut, so I'm sure everyone will know about her before too long."

"Okay, I guess since I'm going out, I can pick up something for myself to wear too. Do you want anything?" I asked as I tied my shoes.

"How about a tube of that pinkish lipstick that I like? You know the kind."

"Sure, Mom, we'll be back a little later on. Oh, wait," I leaned to whisper in her ear. "I almost forgot. I'm taking Leila to my favorite spot in the woods, so we'll be a little while longer. I just don't want you to worry, okay?"

"Thanks for telling me, dear."

I grabbed my purse as Leila bolted for the door. She must have been eager to get out of the house. I picked up my keys and followed her. I opened the front door to see few leaves blowing across the porch. The morning was brisk, but sunny. There was a stray cat walking on the lawn sniffing for something to eat.

As I descended the porch steps, Mom came out the door behind me and I heard the screen door slam shut. I turned to see her carrying a small dish.

"You know, if you feed it, it will keep coming back for more," I informed her.

"And what's wrong with that?" she answered with a smile. The grey cat walked right up to her and began to eat from the bowl. Obviously, Mom had already made a habit of feeding that one. Leila was of course interested in the animal, as kids usually are, and began to pet him. It rubbed on her legs and zigzagged between them. I bent down, joined the two already petting the cat, and was shocked at what I heard. As the cat rubbed its nose on Leila, she giggled. It was quiet, but I heard it nonetheless. It seemed that she was starting to come out of her shell. I hoped that it would not be long before I heard a word from her.

"We better get going now," I said to Leila. She gave the cat a final pat on the head and made her way to the car. We climbed into the front seat and I looked at my mother through the windshield. She sat on the steps with the cat. I began to get nervous as I put the key in the ignition. I was terrified of having another episode while I was in the car. I certainly couldn't stay home all the time though, I thought. I had to keep on living. I did not want to be confined to the house and let my life deteriorate any further.

I started the car up and began my way down the dirt road. Everything seemed fine at that moment. I turned on the music and tried to relax. The gas gage was nearly on empty, but was enough to get to the edge of town. The closest station was just past the limits of our town, about ten minutes away, unless I went five minutes in the opposite direction. There was a station that way, but I didn't want to have to turn back around. I felt sure that I had enough to make it. There were times when that car seemed to go on forever with no gas reading on the gage. That's one of the reasons why I loved it so much.

We drove until I saw the gas station coming into view on the right side. I pulled up to an empty pump and got my credit card out of my wallet.

"Wait here for a minute," I told Leila as I emerged from the car.

I began to fill the tank up and watched the people around me. There were two women sitting in a car in front of the store. They looked as if they were arguing back and forth. The one had her arms waving around over her head and the other had her hand to her forehead. Two spaces over from them was a girl and what I assumed was her father. He was directing her on how to back out and pull out from the gas station. She must have been learning to drive.

I watched the girl and heard my name called from behind me. I turned my head to see where it came from and saw a man.

"Hello, Kate. How are you?" he asked.

"Fine, Dr. Kensington. How are you this morning?" I asked as I began messing with my hair. I got very nervous at the sight of him.

"I am doing just fine. I was on my way to the office and I saw you, so I thought I would say hello. I live near here, so this is my first stop in the mornings. I get coffee, gas, and off I go."

"I had no idea you lived this far out from the city."

"It's a long commute, but I enjoy the drive. Well, it has been nice seeing you Kate. I've got to get going now."

"You too, doctor."

I escaped the chilly air as I sat back in the car. Dr. Kensington sure was a good-looking man. Maybe he was interested in me, I thought. I then remembered what he knew. He knew all there was to know about my mental health. I was fairly certain that dependent women with no job and the added bonus of memory loss were not a turn-on for most men. I glanced to the rear-view just in time to see him returning to his car. He had walked across the entire parking lot just to say hello. Maybe he had been a slight bit interested. If nothing else, at least I got the pleasure of watching him stroll away.

I returned my focus to the task at hand. I was in pursuit of a wardrobe for Leila and a new outfit for myself. Maybe even a new top to wear to my next appointment with the good doctor. I headed down the road in the direction of a shopping plaza that I frequented quite often. Multiple department stores there always had great deals on everything.

The lot was almost completely empty when we arrived. It was still early and the stores were just opening. Besides that, it was only Wednesday. Most people were at work, not out shopping.

Leila and I got out of the car and began walking to the first department store. I noticed a man with a push broom going up and down the sidewalk in front of the building. He smiled as we walked past and continued with his work. I thought of when I was younger. I worked at a small clothing store near Mom's house when I turned sixteen. It was the first job I had ever had. I made only minimum wage and did a lot a sweeping the floors, but the idea of having my own money was what made me work. I put in long hours, after school and on weekends. I saved almost everything that I ever earned until I had enough to buy my first car. The Le Baron was that car. It was nearly brand new when I got it. Part of the reason why I still had the car was because it still was in working order. Partly, it was because I knew just how hard I had worked to get that car. It would have been as if I was throwing away all of that effort if I got another one.

That particular clothing store no longer remained where it had been all those years ago. The building was empty for a few months when the shop went out of business, and then a tobacco outlet leased the space.

We entered into the bright lights and white aisles of the store, not knowing which direction to go. A woman wearing a store vest asked if she could help us and then pointed us in the direction of the girls' department. We came upon racks of brightly colored clothes and stylish jeans that I had never seen. There were flared jeans and bellbottoms, flashy chains and scarves hanging from skirts, and other pieces that looked more as if they were made for adults. I hoped that everything wasn't like that. I pictured little girls wearing cutesy outfits in pinks and purples with animals on the fronts. Things certainly had changed since I had been young.

To my content, Leila showed no interest in the clothes we first encountered. Her fingers poked through racks and hangers until she finally pulled out a top. It was a light blue, long-sleeve shirt with a small ruffle around the bottom. It was plain, but pretty, I thought. She held it up to show me and I nodded in approval. I would not have refused, had she picked out something that I did not care for. After all, it was supposed to be fun and I certainly didn't want to upset her. She continued to look around and ended up with only four articles of clothing. They were the blue top, a pair of jeans with a butterfly embroidered at the bottom, a green plaid skirt, and a hooded pink sweatshirt that had "GIRLZ" sewn on the front in large letters.

I took Leila to the fitting room so she could try the clothes on and sat on a metal chair outside the dressing room door.

"Come out and show me when you're dressed," I called in to her.

I sat and waited. The entire fitting room area had mirrors on all the walls. I stood and looked at my own outfit in the mirror. I put my hands on my hips and moved from side to side as I reviewed my appearance. I was fairly attractive, I thought. Perhaps I could work up enough courage to ask the doctor out on a date. I certainly was not ugly, in my opinion. As

I looked myself over, I caught a glimpse of something on the floor. I kneeled down and picked it up. It was a silver cat pin; rhinestones took the place of the eyes. It must have fallen off clothing that someone had brought back to try on at one time.

I remembered having something just like it once, but could not pinpoint where I had gotten it. I thought of my great aunt Goldie. When she had been alive, she always wore tacky broaches and gaudy jewelry. Anything that was ugly to most people, she thought was gorgeous. An image of the pin came into my mind, only it had rhinestones adorning the tail also. I remembered it more clearly the longer I thought. Then, the image suddenly faded from my mind and a sharp pain in my chest took its place. The pain increased and I felt a strong pressure. The pressure was intensely heavy, as if a boulder had been set atop of me. I could feel the needle as it pushed into my skin. My mouth fell open as I gulped in a breath of air. I raised my hand to my chest. I lifted my shirt in front of the mirror and saw a small red dot on my chest where I had felt the pain. A small drop of blood ran from it and onto my finger as I touched the spot.

I heard the door open behind me and spun around to see Leila wearing the green skirt with the light blue top. I turned my eyes quickly to my finger and saw that there was no blood. The pin was again on the floor. I rubbed my eyes and tried to pretend there was nothing wrong, but Leila was smart, and I knew it. She could tell something was amiss and tilted her head as she looked at me.

"That is so cute!" I complimented her on the outfit, trying to avoid an uncomfortable moment. "You look adorable. Oh, wait, girls probably don't want to hear that these days. You look beautiful! How's that instead?"

She pranced in front of the mirror and spun around in full circle. She obviously knew how great she looked.

"I love that one," I told her. "Try on the other things and let me see."

She returned to the other side of the dressing room door and proceeded to try the next outfit. She seemed to forget all about the strange look I was wearing when she emerged from the room moments ago.

With Leila out of sight again, I flopped myself back onto the chair and tried to reassure myself that I wasn't crazy. I didn't black out or fall asleep, so was it just a dream, or something else? I was fully aware and standing up, nonetheless. I had stood there for mere moments. I thought of my trip to Dr. Kensington's office the other day. I was sure that my next appointment was on Thursday, which was the next day. He would think I was crazy for sure, if he hadn't already, I thought. I peered under my shirt at where the spot had been. This time I saw nothing. These dreams, or visions, or whatever they were, were getting stranger every time one occurred. Nothing made even the slightest bit of sense.

I tried to put everything out of my mind for the rest of the morning, so that I could shop with Leila and have a good time. It was hard, but I did not want to ruin her day because my mind had been somewhere else. She had enough of her own worries, I thought. She certainly did not need to have anything else weighing on her mind. We finished up in the store we were in and went to another. The building next door was a shoe store. The only shoes she had were the mud stained ones she was wearing when I found her. I did not expect her to wear a brand new skirt without nice shoes, so we went in to shop.

As Leila was trying on clothing in another store, I glanced through the women's section, which was right beside the dressing rooms. I found a navy blue, button-down satin top for myself. It was just a little bit sexy, but nothing too revealing. I waited until Leila had finished in the fitting room, and we went to the make-up counter before leaving. I had almost forgotten about my mother's lipstick. I glanced around until I found "pink passion", the lipstick color she always wore. I got myself a tube of gloss, paid, and left the store.

We continued shopping for quite some time until I heard Leila's stomach growl as we left yet another department store. I was shocked as I glanced at my watch.

"Wow! I didn't realize we had been out for so long already. Let's stop and get a bite to eat to hold us over until we get home. Mom will have something good made, I'm sure."

Leila liked the idea of food and nodded her head in agreement.

We loaded our purchases up in the car and pulled up in a drive-through lane at a fast food restaurant. We each got a box of chicken nuggets and a cola, and then headed down the road toward Mom's house. The trip had been very productive. Leila had found numerous outfits and two pairs of shoes. I had gotten a blouse to wear to Dr. Kensington's office the next day, not to mention, another strange story to tell him as well.

As I drove, I couldn't help but think of the pin. I had no idea where I had gotten it or why it had come to mind. I hated the idea of telling my mom about yet another incident, but thought that she might be able to give me some kind of information on the pin.

Leila sat next to me gazing at her feet. She had put her new shoes on while in the car and couldn't take her eyes off of them.

Before we reached the dirt road, we came upon another road off to the left. It was where I had wanted to take Leila to see one of my favorite spots. I often went there when I was a few years younger to sit and unwind. Nature has always been so relaxing to me. I pulled down the road until we came to the end and there was nowhere further to go by car.

"I want to show you something before we go back to the house. I think you'll really like it. I always enjoy coming out here," I turned to her and said.

I parked the car and stepped out onto the grass beside the door. I took in a deep breath of the fresh air. For some reason, it seemed different from the air at home, even though it was so close. Leila and I walked hand in hand down a small path through the trees. The leaves and twigs crunched under our feet as we made our way. She swung her arm with mine and skipped as she went. She was just as much of a nature lover as I was, I thought. She always looked so happy when we were outside.

The trees rustled and I saw movement in them. I turned to my right to see a large doe standing about thirty feet away from us. I stopped and crouched down to Leila's level. She had already spotted it and was standing completely still. It stood for a moment and then took off in an instant.

We continued down the path until we came to the end where we heard running water. We walked up a small hill and, when we reached the top, stood just over a small waterfall. We were on a rock that looked out over a small creek. There was enough room for three people to sit comfortably on it and look down over the edge. We could not see the water falling from there, but we could hear it, and see the water ripple down below. It was only a small drop down to the water. I had often jumped into it to cool down in the summertime. Mostly, though, I just enjoyed sitting there, listening to the sounds. It took me away to a place where nothing mattered, and none of my problems seemed important.

That day, there was a nest of birds, in plain view, in a tree on the other side of the water. We sat atop the rock and watched them. I could not tell how many birds were in the nest, but they were chirping for their dinner.

I looked to Leila and saw her picking up pebbles beside her. She tossed them one by one over the edge. She waited until she heard the "plop" from one before tossing the next.

"This is a very special place to me. When I was little, I liked to come here because no on else knew where I was. I had never seen anyone else out here so I felt as if it were my very own spot. Some kids had tree houses, but I always had this."

We sat for about half an hour on the rock. Leila wasn't antsy to get up and sat very quietly, taking in all the sounds and sights of the woods. I sucked up as much of the air as I could before standing. The smell was incredible. I wished I could bottle it up and reopen it when I needed a pick-me-up. I was so glad to have shared that time with Leila in that spot, even if only for a brief time. I wanted her to know that I cared about her, and hopefully, by sharing this place with her, she felt that.

We pulled up to the house around one o'clock. The old truck that my father drove was not there. I assumed that we had just missed him. He usually came home for lunch around a quarter after twelve.

"Mom, we're back," I called as we stepped into the kitchen. "Sorry we weren't back in time for lunch."

"That's fine girls, just sit down and I'll get you a couple of plates while the food is warming back up in the oven. Did you remember my lipstick?" she asked with a big smile.

"I nearly forgot, but here it is," I said as I handed it to her. She only wore one shade of lipstick, and it had been that way for as long as I could remember. Of course, it looked fabulous on her, so she had no reason to change.

I wondered if I should tell her about what had happened at the store. I did not want to give her anything more to worry about, and yet I was curious about the pin I had seen. Maybe if I told her, she would know what significance the pin held, and why it had come to mind. After a few minutes, I decided that I would research it myself first. If I found nothing, I would go to her. If it was in the house somewhere, I could find it. There were only so many places to look.

"What time does the banquet start tomorrow?" I asked, changing my thoughts.

"Oh, we're not going to go," Mom stated.

"Why not? I thought you were making food for it?"

"Well, I am going to send my dish with Mrs. Flynn, but I don't feel much like attending."

"But you wanted to go earlier. Did something happen?"

"It's just not going to work, Kate! It's not a big deal, I just don't think it's a good idea anymore! There will be a lot of people there and I don't want to make Leila uncomfortable."

"She seems fine with meeting new people, Mom."

"That's not it, I, I've made my decision and I don't want to go. Now that's the end of it," she stated firmly.

Mom had a sad look on her face. I knew that she enjoyed the few social activities that she normally attended. It gave her a chance to get out a little and talk to her friends. I wondered why she thought that Leila shouldn't meet anyone. She seemed fine with everyone that she had come across to that point. Still, it was not like Mom to change her mind at the last minute. There was something that she was holding back. I didn't want to upset her any further, so I let it go, although I had a feeling that something was not right.

-10-

I sat in the green lounge chair at Dr. Kensington's office patiently, and was a little bit nervous. I had been thinking about him off and on, which was more than I should have been. I didn't actually think I would have the courage to say anything at all to him, and was hoping for him to make the first move. I felt rather childish as I sat and thought about the tall, dark man. It was like being a small schoolgirl who became instantly dumbfounded the second a cute boy came around. I only wanted to ask the doctor out for a cup of coffee, perhaps dinner, and that was all. My only concern, which held me back, was the fact that he was my shrink, and he knew everything there was to know about my past mental state. He knew the things that even I did not know, and that is what worried me. I had no idea of what had gone on during the last year of my life. He probably saw me as a total basket case, I thought, and why would anyone want to date someone like that? Still, I was entertained by the idea of us together.

The scene of the two of us chatting over dinner played repeatedly in my mind as I waited. I imagined him walking through the office door and telling me how he had been thinking of me. My eyes were shut, and I smiled as I thought about Dr. Kensington, Steven.

"What has you in such a good mood?"

My eyes popped open and I sat up on the lounge. I had not expected him to be in the room so quickly. Our session wasn't set to start for a few more minutes.

"Oh, doctor, you startled me! I was, um, I was just thinking of yesterday," I lied.

"What was so wonderful about yesterday?" he asked, "and please, call me Steven."

"Well, not much, Steven," I said as he smiled down at me, "I just took Leila shopping for some new clothes. You know, it was really fun too. We had a great time. I think she enjoyed it too."

"That's wonderful. It's great that you two are spending time together. I'm sure it has been just what she needs to keep her mind off of her own worries."

"She seems to be happy most of the time, so I'm not really sure how much she actually remembers about her family or what happened to them. Maybe it's better that way, although I wish I knew where they were."

"That's what I wanted to talk about first today, if that is alright. I want to know more about this little girl."

"Sure, although I don't know how much more I can tell you. I don't know all that much myself."

"Well, for starters, has she told you anything about her mother or father? Has she mentioned either of them in conversation?"

"Actually," I began with a sigh, "she hasn't said anything about anything."

"What do you mean?"

"She has yet to speak to me. She hasn't said a word to anyone since I took her to my mother's house. I think she is slowly becoming more comfortable with us, because I heard her giggling the other morning. Other than that, I have not heard a single thing from her," I told him.

"Hmmm," he quietly made a noise. "I'm sure she will begin to talk when she is ready, but that doesn't help us to understand her any better. You said she seems to be happy. Are you pretty certain about that?"

"Oh, yeah, she smiles a lot and I haven't seen her cry or anything like that." I stopped to think. "Do you think maybe she's just keeping everything inside?"

"Perhaps, but I wouldn't worry too much about it for now. Just enjoy your time with her and keep her happy. You have no idea when she'll be gone from your life, so enjoy what you have until the very end."

He was right. I wanted her to enjoy every minute of her stay with us. Even so, I couldn't help but wonder what she was thinking. I could only hope that she wasn't crying on the inside. As I laid there thinking, my eyes fell upon a photo of a young boy and what I assumed was his mother.

"Is that your son?" I asked, becoming depressed at the idea of him already having a girlfriend and child.

"Where? Oh, on the wall? No," he answered. "That is actually me when I was about ten years old. That's my mother standing with me."

"Why don't you have something a little more recent? She's not…oh, I'm so sorry," I apologized.

He laughed a little before speaking, "No, don't be. She hasn't passed, she's just not the same anymore, mentally I mean. She became, shall I say, a little less fond of me as I grew older, so I like to remember us the way we were at that exact point in my life. We were quite happy then."

"Oh," I uttered in a low voice. I wasn't sure what to say. "How could anyone not like you?" I said quietly, thinking that I was the only one who would hear.

"You'd be surprised," he said with a chuckle.

I felt my face warming as my cheeks undoubtedly turned red. I hadn't intended for him to hear me.

He scratched some information down on his tablet and was silent. I couldn't see him as I was lying facing the opposite direction of him. I waited for him to speak, but heard nothing for a minute. Finally, he spoke.

"Did you follow my instructions about bringing your dreams to life?"

"I did, actually, and nothing happened. Well, nothing happened until I went back into the house. That's when I noticed something that led to some answers for me," I said as I recalled the painting. "I know about my living arrangements and my inability to remember everything. I feel like such a fool that everyone around me had been keeping it from me. That includes you, doctor." I forgot for a moment that I found him attractive and began to get very angry. "I don't think you should have kept it from me, or asked my mother to keep that from me."

"Now, Kate. When we began seeing each other, we agreed that the best way for you to recover when you have a lapse in memory is to let it come back slowly. I did not want to push anything on you if I did not feel you were capable of handling it. I was only doing it in your best interest. If I would have told you right from the start, you may have acted irrationally."

Irrationally, I thought. He sounded as if he thought I was a maniac, ready to let loose at any moment.

"Now that you know, you can move forward. Things will make more sense as time passes. Trust me. We've been down this road before and each time everything has worked out. Please don't be angry," he said, trying to calm me down.

I began to let go of my anger and tried to relax. It was done and over with, and perhaps he had been right. Maybe it had been best that I learn slowly, although I didn't see how it made it any easier for me.

"So you are aware that you no longer live on your own and that you have forgotten a part of your life. Do you feel as if you no longer have control over your own life? Do you feel as you did before, or do you feel like a different person altogether?"

"That's why this all seems so unbelievable to me. I feel the same as I did before I knew. I don't feel like I've missed anything. It feels more like everyone around me has lost their minds, and I am the same person I always was. My mother has been acting very strange, and that's sort of making everyday life a little bit off track." I watched as he scribbled on his tablet. "My life is as if it has just gone from one day to the next, like everyone else's. I don't recognize where there is a gap when anything doesn't fit together. I'm just trying to take all of this into my mind because that is what I am being told."

"You say that you cannot distinguish the point when your memory had lapsed. Think about the past few days or so and tell me about them. I'm sure if you say where you have been, you will easily be able to identify where your memory faltered," he assured me.

"I remember being in my apartment last Friday. I went out to a club with a girlfriend of mine and returned to my apartment around midnight. Since I was told I've been living at my parents' house for a while now, I guess that wasn't last Friday. I left the house on Saturday and went to the grocery store before heading to Mom's house around noon. I spent that night at her house, woke up on Sunday, and ate breakfast with them. We talked and laughed at the table and had a normal day. I helped Mom clean up a little around the house and Dad worked out in the yard, cleaning up leaves and things. I stayed there most of the day and headed home after dinner. That's the night I came across Leila."

Dr. Kensington jotted a few things down on his pad. I heard his pencil racing frantically across the paper.

"Somewhere in that space of time, you must have lapsed and not realized. It may have been during that weekend. You may want to check with your mother and verify that things happened as you remember them. That's the best way to determine exactly what has happened recently, and what is from your past."

I thought about what had happened yesterday while shopping with Leila. I had nearly forgotten to mention it.

"Dr. Kensington, there is something else. It was yesterday. I was shopping with Leila, she went to try on some clothing, and something very strange happened. It scared me a little, but then was gone, just as quickly as it had happened."

"What do you mean?" he questioned with concern in his voice.

"Well, this is going to sound crazy, but, oh never mind."

"Tell me, please. I won't think you're a lunatic, if that's what you're worried about. You wouldn't believe the kinds of stories I hear from people in here. I'm sure yours isn't any worse." The look on his face showed that he was sincere, and I decided to continue opening up to him.

"I had a memory of a pin, like a broach, and then, immediately after, I felt a weight on my chest. It was the creepiest thing. I even felt pain from the pin's needle piercing me and saw the blood on my chest when I checked under my shirt. I touched it, but then it disappeared just like that," I explained to him. A quiver ran down my spine. "I'm getting chills just thinking about it!"

"That is strange. I'll give you that much. Well, what do you remember about the pin? Can you put it together with any particular memory or person?" he questioned further.

"I can only remember seeing it at one time, and that is all. I don't remember ever wearing it or even where it came from. Have I completely lost my mind or is there some way that this could have really happened?" I must have sounded so desperate, which probably was less than a turn-on.

"No, you have not lost your mind, Kate. Our minds have their own ways of communicating things to us when something is important. It may seem as if it was real and the blood may have seemed real, but our subconscious can be very persuasive. Your mind is trying to have you remember something that is of extreme importance. Until you figure out what that is, you may continue to experience these strange occurrences. My best advice is what you already know. Continue to do as you already have. Make it real, if possible. Try to locate the pin you saw and move forward from there."

Not again, I thought. I needed more help than what he was giving me. I wanted answers, and I did not want to wait for them.

"Isn't there anything else you can tell me? What if I come up empty-handed? What if there is no trace of that pin? Then what will I do?" I pleaded to him.

"We will cross that bridge when we come to it. Also, enjoy your time with Leila. Try to find out what she really likes. Then, maybe she'll open up to you a little. Now, we are through for today so I will see you again in a few more days. Okay?"

"All right, doc," I replied as I sat up straight and looked at him. His eyes were a gorgeous deep brown and he smelled of expensive cologne, not too much, but just enough.

"Dr. Kensington," I spoke, not even knowing why. I did not plan to actually ask him out. I was at a loss for words and sat there looking stupid.

"Yes," he said as he turned to me.

"Oh, never mind." There was an uncomfortable silent pause. I wondered if he knew what I wanted to say. He stood where he was, and after a moment, a small grin appeared on his face. He took a few steps back in my direction.

"Kate," he paused as if he were suddenly nervous also, "would you like to have a cup of coffee with me this afternoon?"

I was speechless. I never expected him to be the one to ask me.

"I have an empty afternoon today and I thought that maybe you would join me at the café down the street, that is if you don't already have plans."

"Yeah, you bet!" I blurted out eagerly; unaware of how stupid I must have sounded. "That would be nice," I tried to calm down my tone. "What time would you like me to meet you?"

"How about one thirty at the café on the corner? Bring Leila if you'd like. I would love to meet her."

"Okay, that sounds great! I'll see you then." I smiled as he left the room. I could not believe he had been interested in me. I slung my purse over my arm and sauntered out to make another appointment with the secretary. I suddenly felt very sexy and alive. I had never been as ecstatic about a cup of coffee as I was at that moment.

-11-

The sky looked bluer than ever as we drove downtown. There were white puffy clouds, just as they would look if someone had painted them in the sky. The air was cool, but comfortable. I leaned back in the car seat as we waited at the traffic light. I could smell buns baking at the bakery to my left. The sights of the city were gorgeous, seeing all the skyscrapers covered in mirrors and the busy people rushing down the sidewalks. I loved to see it, but hated the thought of being a part of all the hustle and bustle. It was way too much for my personal taste.

As I waited, I thought of my conversation with Mom after I returned from my appointment that morning. She didn't seemed surprised much when I told her that the doctor had asked me to coffee. She only gave a grin and told me how much she liked his appearance. She mentioned that she had always thought that he might have been a bit interested. When I asked her why she thought that, she commented on how he had always asked about me when she ran into him at various places.

"I saw him on occasion at the grocery store and he always asked how you were doing and whether you were dating or not," she told me earlier that day.

"But you never said anything!" I had said to her.

"He said he would work up the nerve sooner or later, and asked me not to mention it," she had confessed.

I was so excited, yet I was so nervous. I never dated much and was an amateur at it. Never had I gone out with someone so good-looking. I thought for sure that he was out of my league.

Leila sat next to me in her new jeans and pink hooded shirt. She had her hair done in two pigtails with light blue ribbons. She was happy to be out of the house that day. I could tell that by the way she leaned toward the window. She looked like she was about to leap right out.

I glanced at the clock. It was twenty after one. The café was only another block away. I hoped that Dr. Kensington hadn't been there early, waiting too long. I reached the parking lot of the café and found an empty space. Checking in the mirror, I ran my fingers through my hair and dabbed some gloss on my lips. I wanted to look my best, as I wore a pair of dressy black slacks and boots. A chocolate brown sweater covered the top of me and a matching belt tied loosely around my waist. I did not want to seem too dressed up, and so chose not to wear a skirt. At the same time, I hoped that he did not find me underdressed and take offense.

I rounded the corner of the café with Leila on my right side and spotted out the doctor right away. I stopped Leila for a moment. I just needed to take a deep breath. It was incredible how anxious I felt after merely glancing at him. He wore a dark green sweater and black leather jacket with a pair of light colored khakis. I was relieved to see that his attire seemed to be of the same standing as mine. He looked incredible, I thought as I resumed my walk over to his table. He sat at a small round table on the patio of the café. He sipped on a cup of coffee as he read the newspaper. As he lowered the cup, he turned in our direction and saw the two of us approaching.

"Well hello ladies," he said as he rose from his seat. "It's wonderful to see you again Kate."

"Nice to see you as well, Dr. Kensington," I replied.

"Didn't I tell you to call me Steven?" he said with a smile. "And this must be the beautiful Leila that I have heard so much about," he spoke as he lowered himself down to her level.

She smiled and offered her hand for a shake. He put his hand in hers for a moment and then returned the smile.

"Kate told me that you were a pretty girl, but I had no idea you would be this beautiful. It is very nice to meet you, my dear." He rose back up and spoke to me again. "Can I get you a latte or cappuccino, Kate?"

"A latte would be great, thanks."

"And for you, Leila, hot chocolate," he said as he turned into the building. "Have a seat and I'll be right back."

Leila licked her lips at the thought of hot chocolate and climbed onto a chair at the table. I took a seat next to her and waited. The newspaper was opened up to the real estate classified section. Had he been planning to buy a new home, I wondered. He probably earned enough money with his career to afford quite an exquisite home.

"Here we are," he said cheerfully as he returned from the café counter. He put down a large cup in front of me, and a child's size mug next to Leila. "Now be very careful. I'm sure that is very hot."

"Thank you, Steven," I said awkwardly. It sounded strange as it rolled from my lips. I was accustomed to calling him by Dr. Kensington. I tried to think of a conversation starter, but drew a blank. Fortunately, Steven did not appear to be as nervous as I was.

"Have you ever come to this café before?" he asked.

"No, I haven't. I don't come into the city too much. I have never cared much for the traffic in big cities. It makes me a little nervous because drivers that are in a rush don't have any regard for other people's safety."

"That's completely understandable. I don't care much for it either, but with my job, I had to adjust to driving in town. I often come to this place, though. They have the best drinks around and everyone here has always been so nice to me."

Of course, they would be nice to you, I thought. With a face like his, the entire world would kiss your feet.

"Are you looking to buy a house?" I asked, glancing toward the newspaper.

"Oh, yes, at some point, but I'm not altogether certain where I want to live. I don't really want to travel far to get to my office, but yet I like the idea of going home to a quite place away from the city for the night. You know, somewhere on the outskirts of town. My place now is out of town a ways and I like it. It just isn't mine. I haven't decided yet, but I'm leaning toward staying in the same vicinity I am in now. What I'd really like is to be on a quiet country road all my own. I think I would be willing to continue the forty-five minute commute if I could find a nice place like that."

"You already travel that far?" I asked, remembering seeing him at the gas station the day before.

"Yes. I live outside of town, about forty minutes or so from my office. It's not bad, but there is still a good bit of traffic along my road. I want to have a drive all to myself, where there is virtually no traffic, and all you can hear is the sound of the bugs."

"My mother's place is like that. Of course, it is by no means a fancy house, but it is away from all the hustle of the road. The drive back to her house is a dirt road that no one else uses."

"That sounds wonderful." He looked down to the paper. "Until I decide exactly what I want, I am going to keep my eyes open to see what is available. Something will become available that will catch my eye sooner or later." He rolled up the paper and set it to the side. "Well, that's enough about me. Tell me a little bit about you. I would love to know all there is about you."

"Well, I'm not sure if I can. You probably know everything there is to know about me, but I'll try." I tried to think of something that I probably had never told him about in our discussions. I thought about photography. There seemed to be no reason why I would have ever spoken to him about that. "I love taking pictures," I began. "I became a photographer right out of school. I took an interest in it at a young age and was lucky enough to have gotten hired right away for various jobs."

"How did you get started in that?" he questioned.

"My mother was always playing with a camera when I was little and I followed behind her. I was just as interested in it as she was. She showed me how to use a camera and how to take great shots." I smiled as I pictured it in my mind. Mom was always taking pictures of me when I dressed up, and when I pretended to be a princess. "My favorite places to photograph are ones in nature, like waterfalls and meadows of flowers. It makes me feel at peace, as if nothing else in the world matters, just for those few moments."

"That's amazing, Kate. You must be wonderful at what you do to be able to do it professionally. I hear that some artists, such as photographers, sometimes can find it hard to get a foot in the door and become professionals. I'm glad you have something that you enjoy. You sound very passionate about it."

"I guess I must have a knack for it. All it took for me was taking a portfolio of some of my work to a magazine company. They loved my shots and hired me for various photo shoots. I was pretty lucky to get into work so quickly."

I thought about my camera sitting under the house and became a little sullen. "I just realized the other day that I had stopped taking pictures, for some reason, but I am going to start again. It's what I love, so I just don't see any good reason for quitting."

We continued talking for at least an hour. Leila was content to sit and listen while we chatted. Once we had gotten started, it seemed much easier than I expected to find things to say. He was very easy to talk to and seemed to enjoy our conversation as well. Halfway through our talk, he got up to get Leila another cup of hot chocolate and brought her back a muffin that was too big even for an adult to eat entirely. The afternoon was perfect, I thought. There I was, having coffee with the most gorgeous man who had ever asked me out for a drink. The weather was perfect and my life wasn't looking quite so bad, in spite of my problems. I would repeat the afternoon over again if it were possible.

"Well, I guess I had better return to the office. I have an appointment this afternoon that I cannot miss. My secretary kind of sprung it on me at the last minute. I'm sorry we couldn't have had more time." He gathered up his newspaper and looked at me once again. "I had a great time Kate. It was a real pleasure spending time with you and Leila."

"It was nice, Steven. Thank you for inviting us out, and thanks for the drinks as well," I said as I looked into his eyes.

"I would like to get together again soon, if you feel the same," he said.

"Of course, that would be great." I wrote my cell phone number down on a napkin that sat on top of the table. As I handed it to him, I said, "My phone is always with me, so anytime is fine."

"Great! I'll be in touch. It was wonderful to meet you Leila," he ended our talk and headed for the corner. When he got to the edge of the building, he turned around briefly and waived back at us. His office was only across the street on the next block.

Leila and I got up and headed for the car. The afternoon could not have gone any better. We pulled out of the parking lot and headed home. I was so excited to tell my mother about our afternoon with Dr. Kensington. What made it even more thrilling was the fact that he wanted to see me again. I must not have bored him over coffee, I thought, or else he wouldn't have asked to see me another time. I couldn't help but wonder though, why he had not asked me out sooner, if I had in fact been seeing him professionally for quite some time. As I thought, I realized that maybe he had been just as shy and nervous to ask as I was.

We pulled onto the dirt road leading to the house. The day was still sunny and gorgeous. The leaves were changing colors rapidly as October ended, and the evergreens stood out more than ever. I knew that once the trees were covered with snow, it would be a truly beautiful sight. Every winter, the house looked as if it were something right off a canvas. The trees and snow were perfectly placed around the house, and the spouting carefully kept icicles in place.

I grabbed my purse and went into the house after Leila. I could immediately smell the pinch-me cake that sat on the countertop cooling.

"Hey, Mom, we're back," I announced as I walked into the kitchen. I swung my purse and walked with bounce in every step.

"Hello girls. How was your afternoon with that gorgeous man?"

"It was amazing, Mom! I couldn't believe it! I was surprised at how easy it was to talk to him outside of his office. I was afraid that it would be awkward, but it wasn't at all. That's not even the best part! He must not think that I am totally crazy or boring because he said that he wanted to see me again! Isn't that wonderful?" I blurted out. I could not hold in my excitement.

"Maybe I'll get to be a mother-in-law to a handsome, wealthy man," said Mom.

"Whoa, now slow down Mom. It was only a cup of coffee. Don't plan on marrying me off just yet."

I reached for a piece of the cake on the countertop. It was still warm, and that was the best way to eat it.

"Is this for us, Mom?" I asked eager to take a chunk.

"Sure is. Go ahead and have some," she replied.

I took three plates from the cupboard and placed them on the table. I sat the cake on the table and sat next to Leila. Her eyes grew large as I placed a piece onto the plate in front of her.

"Are you having some now, Mom?"

"Are you kidding? Of course I am! If I want some, I have to get it now before your father comes home and discovers that I baked this. You know this is one of his absolute favorites," she answered as she pinched a piece of the warm cinnamon cake.

"Did your appointment this morning answer any questions for you?" asked Mom.

"No, but I was so excited about the coffee that I don't remember too much of our conversation. I do recall one thing, though." I thought of the pin. "I'll tell you about it later. I don't want to mention it now. It's nothing big," I said.

-12-

"Mom, thanks for dinner. I'm going to head out now. I'll see you later, all right?" I called to my mother. "I forgot my coat so I'm going to borrow your sweater with the silver broach on the front."

"Okay, hon. Give me a call soon."

The screen door slammed behind me as I walked off the front porch to my car. The moon was shining in the night sky and there was a slight wind. I looked up at the three stars I saw above me and smiled. Mom's home cooking always had a way of making me feel warm and happy. I took my keys from my pocket and reached for the door handle. I paused and looked around me. There was a rustling of branches off in the woods. I figured there were probably deer walking out back behind the house, as they usually did at night.

I slid into the driver's seat of my car and turned the key, followed immediately by turning the radio knob. I hated to drive in silence during the night. It gave me too much time to think, and for a woman too old to be afraid of the dark, that was not a good thing. I overlooked my seatbelt, as I sometimes did, and took off down the dirt road. I came to the end where the dirt met the pavement of the main street, and pulled to the side. I had told my mom that I would put her mail in the box for the mail carrier to pick up the next day. Had I forgotten, her electric bill may have been paid late.

I looked to the passenger seat. There were three envelopes with stamps already affixed to them. The electric bill, a get-well card for a friend of my mother's, and a reply envelope for a flower magazine contest were the three to send. I grabbed them in my right hand and opened the car door with my other. I got out of the car and rounded the door to the mailbox. I hadn't been able to park close enough to avoid getting out because I knew there were flowers still growing there. I didn't want to run them over when they were so successful at extending their lives this late in October. I reached to the box, opened it up, and slid the mail inside. After flipping up the little red flag on the side of the mailbox, I turned back to my car.

I got right beside the door when I felt a hard blow to my head. I crashed to my knees and then to my chest. I felt the pressure of the pin piercing into my skin as I was pushed into the ground. The assailant grabbed me by the sides of my arms and flipped me onto my back with a pair of very strong, large hands. My vision blurred at first and I could only make out the shape of someone on top of me. I tried to push the person off me, but was so overcome with the pain throbbing in my head that I could do nothing. I screamed as my assailant threw my arms down to the ground and held them tight with one hand while searching me with the other. I assumed he was looking for jewelry as he felt around my neck and pushed my hair away from my ears.

"Is there money in your purse?" he screamed at me.

"Yes, just take it. Please don't hurt me," I begged to him between sobbing and screaming. My body trembled as I lay on the cold ground. I only hoped that my life would be spared and that the attacker would be satisfied after obtaining my money and possessions.

The man hovered over me, checking for valuable items. He was so close that I could smell his papaya shampoo. I clenched my eyes shut and prayed that it would all be over soon. I had not seen a single headlight pass by on the main road. This man could kill me, I thought, and not a soul would know about it. My hands grasped tightly at the grass near my fingertips and I waited, shaking. I felt his hand grab my jaw and turn my face to the side, as if he was deciding my worth. His fingers sunk deep into my skin. They were sure to leave a visible mark.

I heard the sound of a semi-truck coming from the distance. The attacker must have heard it also and scrambled to finish his assault on me. He reached for the same bat that he had struck me with earlier and raised it over my head. Tears rolled from my eyes as I begged with the man as he held his weapon above me. I heard him whisper something to me as he held his position. With a final scream, I saw the bat rushing at me and then everything went black.

As the world around me slowly came back into view, I noticed that it was still dark, and I was standing in front of the mailbox. I turned to either side of me and saw no one. My heart pounded fiercely and I choked on my own breath. I raised my hand to my head. There were no bumps or blood, as if nothing had happened. I looked behind me. My car was not there. The tall weeds stood straight up around me. If there had been a struggle, surely the grass would have been pressed to the ground. Had I walked, I wondered. I remembered telling my mother that I would get the mail for the day. She had forgotten to pick it up. I didn't think it had been this dark when I left the house. My mind was a little confused as I walked back toward the house. As I walked, I slowly began to remember things. I had gone for coffee with Steven that day. Leila had gone with me. I remembered talking to Mom about it and then helping her get dinner started. My mind raced as I recalled every detail about what had just happened in my mind. The attack had not been a dream. I remembered it clearly, as if it had happened yesterday. It was as real as my coffee date. It had actually happened at one time, and the idea that I could forget something so traumatic and so frightening scared me ever further. I wondered why it had just then come back to me. Perhaps it was because I stood at the mailbox.

My legs felt heavier than usual as I walked quickly down the dirt road. My walk became a jog, and finally, a full-blown run. The air whipped past my ears and I grew colder. The air was not extremely cold, but I was so afraid that I shivered endlessly. The road seemed shorter than ever as I saw the porch come into view. I must have run incredibly fast to reach the house so soon. The steps slammed under my feet as I climbed up them to the porch and to the door.

I threw the door open and slammed it shut behind me. My lungs were aching as I tried to calm down. My hair was frazzled from the wind blowing in it and my face was flushed. I stood with my back against the door, trying to catch my breath. Mom heard me come in and spoke as she neared the kitchen.

"Kate, do you really have to be so loud? I was watching…" she stopped when she saw me at the door. "Oh, Kate, what happened" Are you all right? Do you need a doctor? Kate, please say something!"

I just stared at her with my washed out face and huffed. I was just beginning to slow my breathing down but could not yet talk to her. I closed my eyes and took a final deep breath before speaking.

"You knew about this, didn't you?" I asked, scared but angry as well. "You knew this whole time and you didn't say anything to me!"

"What are you talking about? I knew about what?"

"A man attacked me. You should have told me!" I screamed. "How could you not tell me something as important as this?" I pushed forcefully past her and began pacing the length of the hallway.

"Kate, I told you that I wasn't supposed to tell you too much. I had put it out of my mind. Nobody wants to remember something like that!"

"You had to know that I would find out sooner or later! You should have prepared me for this!" I continued screaming. "What were you thinking? Why didn't you tell me?" My anger was fading and my sadness had begun to take over as I burst into tears.

"I knew it would come back to you, I just didn't know when. I should have known that the mailbox might trigger something but I honestly didn't realize it when I sent you for the mail. Kate, I am so sorry! I never wanted you to find out this way! I certainly did not want you to be frightened again," she cried to me. "I am so sorry. I should have realized this would happen but it just slipped from my mind."

"Why is this happening to me?" I cried as I looked to the ceiling. I lowered my head into my hands and continued crying. "I don't know what is going on any more!" I sat down at the kitchen table and grabbed a napkin for my tears.

"Why don't you tell me exactly how you remembered this, Kate? Maybe, now that you know, I can fill in the blanks a little more."

I tried to speak, but could not. The sobbing was too overpowering and I knew I would have to wait until I could calm myself down. We sat at the table for ten minutes. Mom had her arms wrapped around me and I just sat, with my face to the placemat. Finally, I looked up at her.

"I was in my car. I told you that I was going home. We had just eaten dinner. I pulled up to the mail box to send out the electric bill and some other things…" I continued to tell Mom about the attack as I saw it in my mind. She nodded her head as I spoke. Obviously, I had described it as she already knew it had happened. When I finished speaking, she continued the story.

"You were hit in the head pretty hard. You only laid there for maybe five minutes. I forgot to give you something when you left that night, so I called your cell phone. When you didn't answer, I got worried, so I sent your dad out after you. He got to the end of the road, saw you, and brought you back to the house. I called for an ambulance to come and get you while we cleaned you up a little bit here." She seemed to choke up even more as she spoke about that evening.

"Is this why I am having these memory problems, because of the blows to my head?"

"We assume so, but we're not certain."

"You told me I was stressed! You could have told me the truth!" I yelled.

"I couldn't Katie. I just couldn't."

"What about he guy who attacked me? Was he arrested? Does anyone even know who it was?" I was terrified to know that the man got away with it.

"No one knows who the attacker was, Kate, I'm sorry to say. He was never found. Unfortunately, you didn't have anything valuable on. Then they may have been able to trace it at a pawnshop, but that wasn't the case. I'm sorry, but there was nothing we could do," her voice said, disheartened. "Apparently no one saw anything down by the road."

"I heard a truck. Maybe the driver saw something or the person who did it!"

"Honey, the police did everything they could. If someone had witnessed it, I'm sure we would know about it by now." She could see the distressed look on my face as she told me. My tears began to flow heavier.

"How long ago did it happen?" I asked, my voice barely audible.

"It was October nineteenth, Kate. I remember the day exactly."

"Then that is why I have forgotten the past year. My mind blocked out everything that happened from the attack on. That makes sense that I would want to forget about it. Mom, did I already know about this once before, or is the first time I found out about it?"

"You already knew, Kate. Do you remember how I told you that I was expecting you to come back when you came in with Leila that morning?" she asked.

I nodded.

"Well, you knew everything just before that night. It was then that you started forgetting things again. The attack was the initial reason why you started seeing Dr. Kensington. Soon after, you had episodes where you would forget days at a time. It happened a lot, Kate. You have had to revisit this attack over again so many times in your mind. Each time, I have had to let you discover it over again all on your own. The doctor decided that that would be the best way for you, despite how hard it was. I only wish there were something I could do to make it stop. I can only imagine how hard it must be for you to keep going through this."

I thought to myself. Dr. Kensington was right. He said that the lapse probably occurred sometime on Sunday, before I found Leila. I had not yet asked Mom to verify my memory of the days before that night.

"Are you certain that my memory lapsed that day, because I can't tell what occurred recently and what was long ago? To me, I was sitting in my apartment just last week."

"I am positive. You were here on Sunday and we had a normal day. We did everything as usual. We ate and sat around talking. You left here for one reason or another, I am not altogether sure. You had mentioned going to a movie or something, so when you were gone late, I didn't worry too much. I fell asleep on the couch that night, so I didn't have a chance to worry about you until I woke. You were gone in the morning so I figured you went to the store. Then you returned later with Leila and you forgot that you lived here. You were talking about your apartment and things from the past. Did anything happen that you can recall from that night, other than finding Leila?"

"I don't remember anything else. I thought I had left here to go home. Then I found her and went to the hospital. Wait a minute. Sunday was October nineteenth. If I were attacked so long ago, why would I forget everything exactly one year later? This isn't making sense. I can understand why my mind would block it out, but what would make me forget on the anniversary of the attack? I wonder if something else happened that night when I left here that I am forgetting." I thought hard about that night. I could not figure out any point in time when things seemed fuzzy and difficult to remember.

I tried so hard to return to that night in my head. I saw myself, leaving Mom's house, but not as she described. To me, I had just left to go to my apartment. I did not remember anything about going to the movies or about living with my parents. Everything was frustrating me to the point where I thought I was going to scream and rip at my hair. I was so tired of constantly being surprised by yet another downfall in my life. Living with my parents was not so horrible that I could not move on, and the loss of my photography could be regained simply by picking up my camera again and dusting it off. To remember something so traumatizing was a completely different thing. I had to relive a horrible event in my life, and that was hard to overcome. The idea that someone did such a heinous act and got away with it was sickening. He was free, and there I was, left to deal with it for the rest of my life. I wondered how this man could live with himself, especially if he had known about my having to go through it repeatedly. He obviously was a heartless creature, with no conscience or soul. I only wished that he could experience everything that he had thrust upon me.

The kitchen grew colder as time passed. Nights were becoming colder. Mom stood to check the thermostat and returned after adjusting it a few degrees. We sat at the table in silence as I tried to take in everything that had invaded my mind that evening. My life was unraveling right before me. I felt as if I had nothing to hold onto to keep myself steady.

"I'm so scared," I whispered to my mom as we sat. "I don't know myself any more. I thought I was okay up until now, but now, I am so afraid." I leaned my head onto her shoulder and cried softly onto her robe. She gently rubbed my hair and tried to soothe me.

"There, there now. You're going to make it through this, baby. I promise you."

I raised my head from her shoulder and saw black swirls of mascara stained on her robe. She looked down and let out a soft giggle. She kissed my forehead and put her hand on my cheek. I loved my mother so much. She always made me feel better, as mothers do. A simple kiss on my head and I let out a small sigh. A slight bit of relief came over me and I gave her a hug. We stood from the table and walked arm in arm to the living room where my father sat watching the news with Leila.

I plopped down on the loveseat and pulled the afghan down over me. I had just closed my eyes when I felt someone crawling under the blanket next to me. I lifted the blanket up as Leila's head came out from underneath. Once she found a comfortable position, I draped my arm over her and looked to the television. It was so comforting to have her with me. A child's innocence and charm was the best way to take away all the evils of a day, even if only temporarily. I thought to myself about why I had found her on the night when my life took a step backwards. Perhaps it was fate. Maybe I was supposed to find her that night as a means of helping me through my own tough times. I wanted to ease her of her own problems, but perhaps we were meant to help each other.

I ran my fingers through her silky blonde hair and she turned her head to me. She still had not said anything to me, but her face was enough. It said a million things without saying a word. Her eyes told me that she was there for me, and that as tough as things were, it was going to be all right. Her smile was reassuring of her thanks to me for caring for her, as no one else had. When she held my hand, she meant that she felt safe with me. She didn't need to speak if she did not want to, and that was perfectly fine with me.

-13-

When the phone rang at breakfast the next morning, I did not expect to hear Detective Malone's voice on the other end. I had nearly forgotten about him. I had become so accustomed to Leila's presence already that she seemed a normal part of my life.

"Good morning Detective. You are making a habit of these early phone calls."

"I need to talk to you about Leila and it cannot wait," he stated, without as much as a greeting to me.

"Oh, okay. What is it?" I asked.

"I have checked everywhere possible and cannot find anything about her. Her parents have not come forward, but that is not what is the most shocking. There are no records of her birth, not here, not another state, not anywhere. It is almost as if she doesn't exist, and clearly she does. Now, I am quite aware that you want her with you, but I cannot guarantee how long that will be if we don't figure something out soon. We may need you to bring her down to the station for a day or so until we can get some kind of information out of her."

"I'm not going to leave her there overnight, if that's what you're asking detective. She would be too scared, and that certainly won't get her to talk to you or anyone else."

"We have nothing to go on right now. She is our only hope of finding answers. She has got to speak to us."

"No, I'm not going to do that to her. She is comfortable with me, and even I haven't heard her speak. I know that she definitely would not talk to you."

"This is not up for debate, Miss Beach. I am the law and you are not. Now, if you do not comply, I will take her away altogether. Would you like that?" he said, as his voice grew louder.

I imagined my arm going into the phone and coming out on his end. I wanted to slap him in the face for being so inconsiderate of the girl's feelings. He did not care what an interrogation might do to her. He just wanted to get the whole issue solved and get the paperwork off his desk. I already knew that it would be a waste of time taking her down to the station. If I were Leila, I certainly would not talk to the man.

"Maybe we could come up with a compromise, Detective."

"You are not in the position to be making demands, Miss Beach, but for now, I'm listening," he grumbled.

"Well, what if you were to come here and speak to her? You may ask her questions and try to get a response from her. She would be more at ease here. Then, if you can't get her to talk, and you really want her down there, then you may take her to the station. Please, try here first," I asked him, trying not to sound as if I were begging. "I think it would make things easier for everyone involved."

"I suppose I could do that, but I don't want any trouble from you after that. If I need to bring her here, I don't want you giving me a hard time about it. Is that clear?"

"Yes, sir," I hated referring to him that way. He certainly didn't deserve respect, but I wanted him to try my way first.

"How about I come over later on this evening? It will be around six or so. Would that be all right?" he asked.

"That would be fine. We'll see you then." I hung up the phone with a sigh. At least I had held him off for the moment. My stomach began to knot up. I did not want Leila to spend a night at the police station being questioned, but I really did not think that she was going to speak to Malone, be it here or there.

I sat back down to my plate of eggs with cheddar cheese. I looked at Leila and smiled.

"Leila, the police man wants to come over tonight to talk to you about some things. Do you think you can talk to him?"

She had a blank expression on her face. She turned her attention back to her eggs and continued eating.

"Honey, I know it is hard for you, but the police man is trying to find out what happened to you the night I found you. It would help a lot if you could speak to him. Just think about it, please." I knelt down next to her beside her chair and whispered. "We need to find out about your family, sweetie. The police man doesn't know anything about you."

For the first time, I saw sadness from Leila. Her hand stopped moving and the fork held still. A single tear rolled down her cheek. She did not make a move for a moment, and then she stood. The fork clanged on the plate and she took off running up to the room where she slept.

"Kate, why did you do such a thing?" Mom yelled as she ran after Leila.

"I didn't mean to upset her!" I yelled back. I felt horrid. I had no idea that I would upset her that way. I followed Mom to the steps where I heard the quiet sobbing of a little girl.

"Let me see her for a minute, Kate," said my mother as she started up the steps. She had grown attached to Leila also, so I understood why she wanted to comfort her. I sat on the step for a moment while Mom went upstairs. I wondered why she had gotten so upset. Maybe it had been the talk about her family, or because I wanted her to speak with the detective. Either way, I knew that if she wouldn't speak to Malone that evening, she would be truly upset if she was taken to the station.

I sat for a few minutes until I could not wait any longer. I felt terrible and I wanted to apologize. I slowly crept up the steps and toward my old bedroom. I peeked around the corner of the door and saw my mother sitting on the bed. Her arms were wrapped around Leila as she sobbed quietly. I imagined myself when I was little. Whenever I was upset, Mom always held me tightly in her arms until I fell asleep. She was more comforting than the biggest pillow. Once, my pet had died and I was sure that life would never be the same. To a small child, it seemed like the end of the world. Chunky, my overweight golden retriever, was my best playmate. Everywhere that I went, he followed diligently. My trips to the waterfall, where I had taken Leila, were always with my four-legged friend. He never strayed and never ran ahead of me. He had always stayed right by my side. Even at his death, he laid his head on my lap and closed his eyes. That was the last they opened. I had never felt so much sadness at that moment. I cried for days, and every night, I fell asleep in my mother's arms. It was the only that way I could, until I eventually began to cheer up again.

I watched the two as they sat on the bed. I admired my mother so much for being the person she was. I always hoped I would get older and be just like her. She was so loving and compassionate, just as a mother should be. I wished that when my time came to be a mother, I would be with my child the way I remembered her being with me.

"It's okay, sweetheart," Mom whispered. "It's going to take some time for things to get back to the way they should be. It is going to get better, though. I promise you," she told the little girl.

I thought to myself. Perhaps the idea of getting back to her previous life scared her, too. That was always a possibility. Maybe she had been left outside for a reason. If someone had not wanted her anymore, the thought of going back to that person would definitely be disturbing. This all could have very well been why she refused to speak. She may have feared going home.

The door creaked as I pushed it open further and looked into the room. Mom turned in my direction and smiled. There were tears rolling down her cheeks as well. She wiped at them quickly with her sleeve and took in a deep breath. The room was rather warm as I stepped beside the bed. I crouched down and looked into the eyes of the beautiful little girl. She looked lonely and scared. When she looked up into my eyes, I was taken back to the night that I found her by the road. She had the same lost gaze in her eyes. I opened my arms, hoping she would get down from the bed and give me a hug. She sat for a moment, and then slid off my mother's lap. Her arms wrapped around me and she held on tighter than I had ever felt.

"I am so sorry, sweetie. I never meant to upset you. Please forgive me," I softly spoke in her ear as her head lay on my shoulder.

She continued to cry and did not look up at me. As she held me for a few minutes, I realized that she wasn't going to let go. I got up, with her in my arms, and sat down in the rocking chair next to the night table. I sat, holding her in my arms, and let her cry. Whatever she had gone through, prior to meeting me, had had a tremendous effect on her. I knew I had to find out what happened, somehow.

Mom stood from the bed and left the room, pulling the door shut behind her.

We sat in the chair for twenty minutes. As the crying slowly eased up, so did her grip on me. She was quiet and flimsy. When her arms dangled over my shoulders, I realized that she had fallen asleep.

I laid her onto the bed and pulled the covers up over her.

Downstairs on the couch, Mom sat reading the morning paper. I sat with her and began to speak.

"I don't know what to do, Mom. Malone wants to take Leila to the station if he cannot get any information from her when he comes. That is going to be too much for her. She is only five years old. How can he be so cold to a child?"

"Perhaps he does not have any children of his own. He doesn't understand how to deal with them," she answered.

"I don't have any and I know better than that," I said, saddened. "I really feel responsible for her, Mom. I want to keep her safe and happy, and I just don't know how to handle this. I wish she didn't have to go through this, even if it meant that I never would have gotten to meet her. She should be home with a family that loves her and wants the best for her."

"Well, for now, she has us, and I am sure that she is grateful for that."

"If only I could find out something, anything, to tell Malone. Then, maybe he would leave her alone for now. There has got to be a way." I thought for a moment. "Is there any way that she could have been born without some kind of record of it? That seems impossible to me. Have you ever come across anything like this in your time volunteering?"

"Everyone has to be accounted for somehow. There must be something to identify her or her family."

"I have to think. How could I find out about her? I have nothing to go on." I thought of the rainy night on Sunday. "I am going to go out for a few minutes. Do you mind staying here with her please?"